C

Bo
978

Bo
978

Bo
978

Bo
978

Bo
978

Bo
978

Bo
978

Bo
978

Bo
978

Boffin Boy and the Rock Men
978 184167 624 1

Boffin Boy and the Temples of Mars
978 184167 623 4

Boffin Boy and the Forest of the Ninja
978 184167 627 2

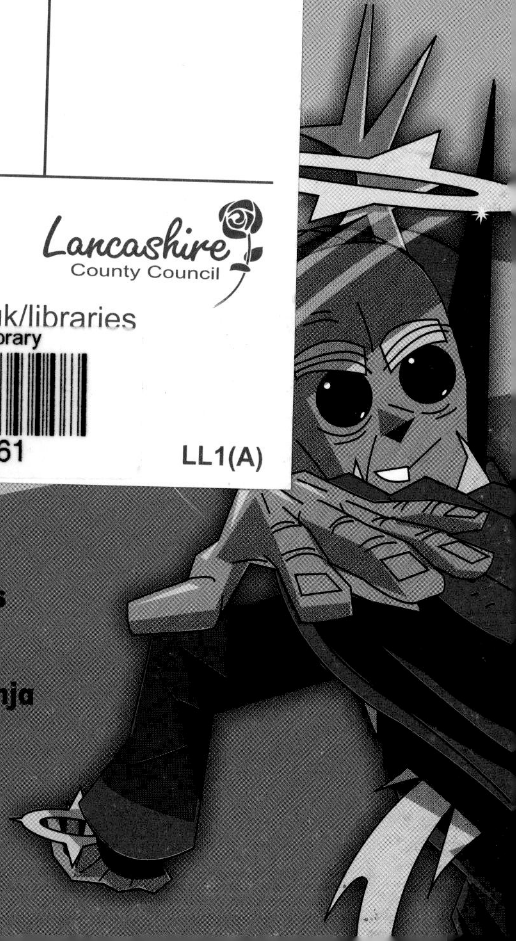

Boffin Boy and the Time Warriors
by David Orme

Illustrated by Peter Richardson

Published by Ransom Publishing Ltd.
51 Southgate Street, Winchester, Hampshire, SO23 9EH, UK
www.ransom.co.uk

ISBN 978 184167 622 7
First published in 2006
Second printing 2007
Copyright © 2006 Ransom Publishing Ltd.

Illustrations copyright © 2006 Peter Richardson

Design & layout: *www.macwiz.co.uk*

Find out more about Boffin Boy at *www.ransom.co.uk*.

Boffin Boy and the Time Warriors

By David Orme

Illustrated by Peter Richardson

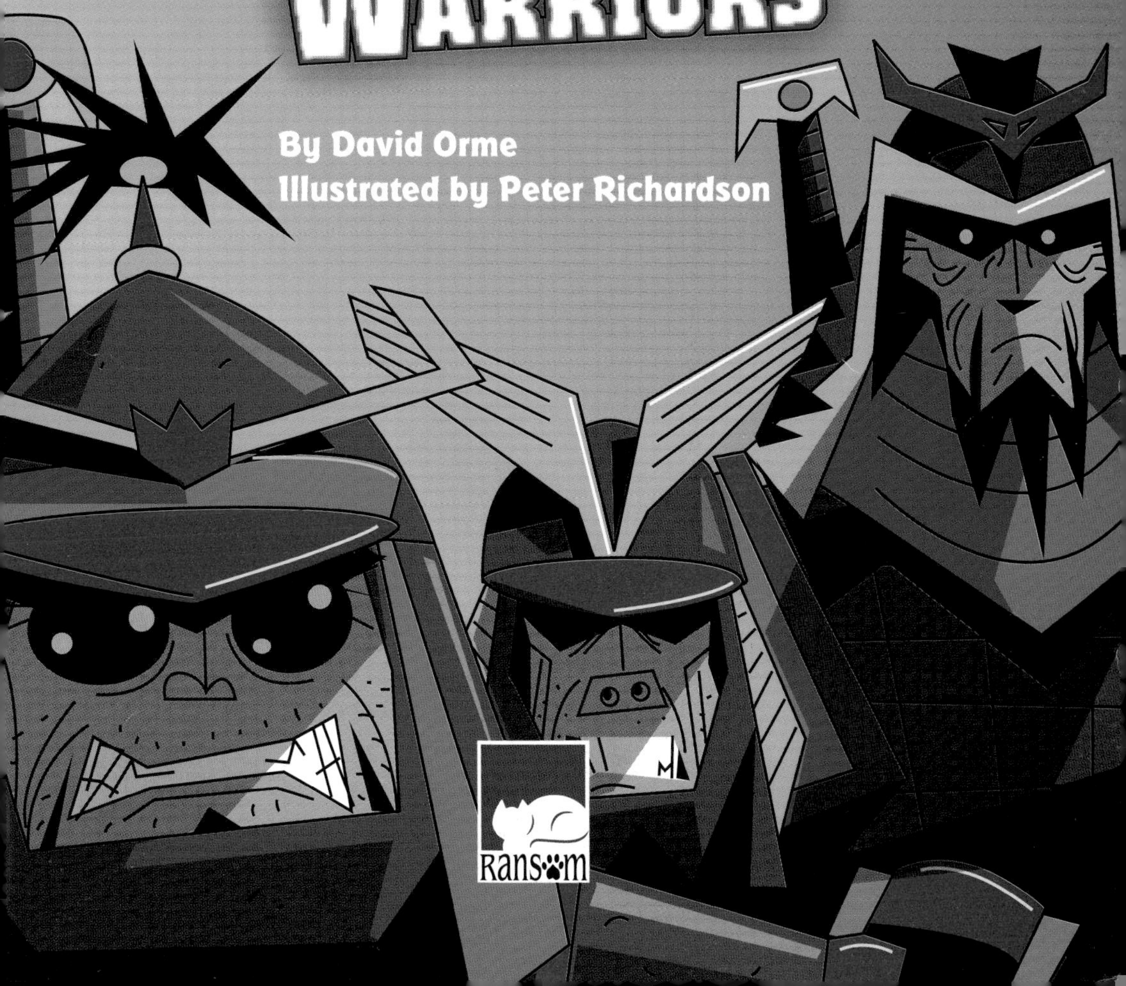

Ransom

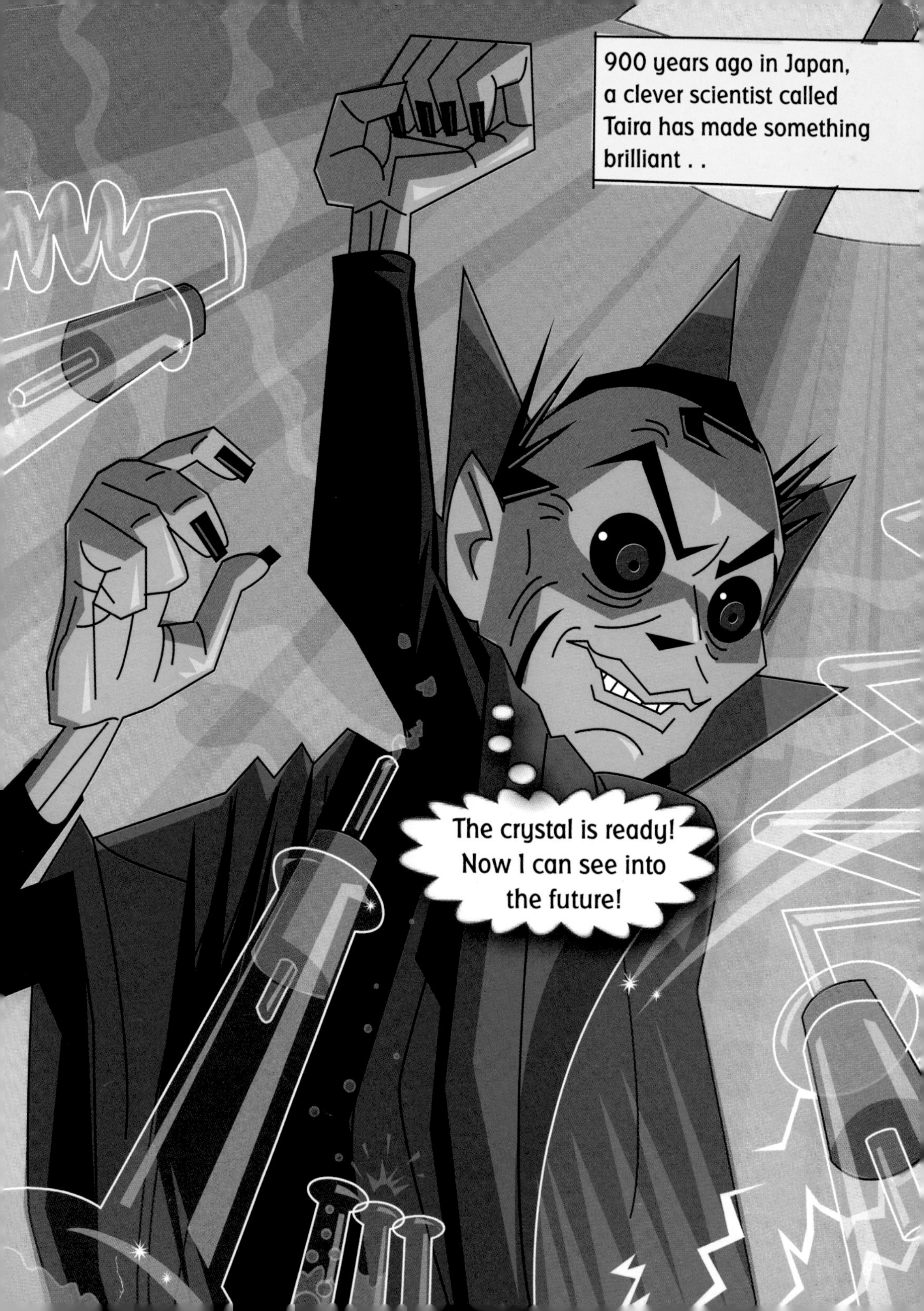
900 years ago in Japan, a clever scientist called Taira has made something brilliant . .
The crystal is ready! Now I can see into the future!

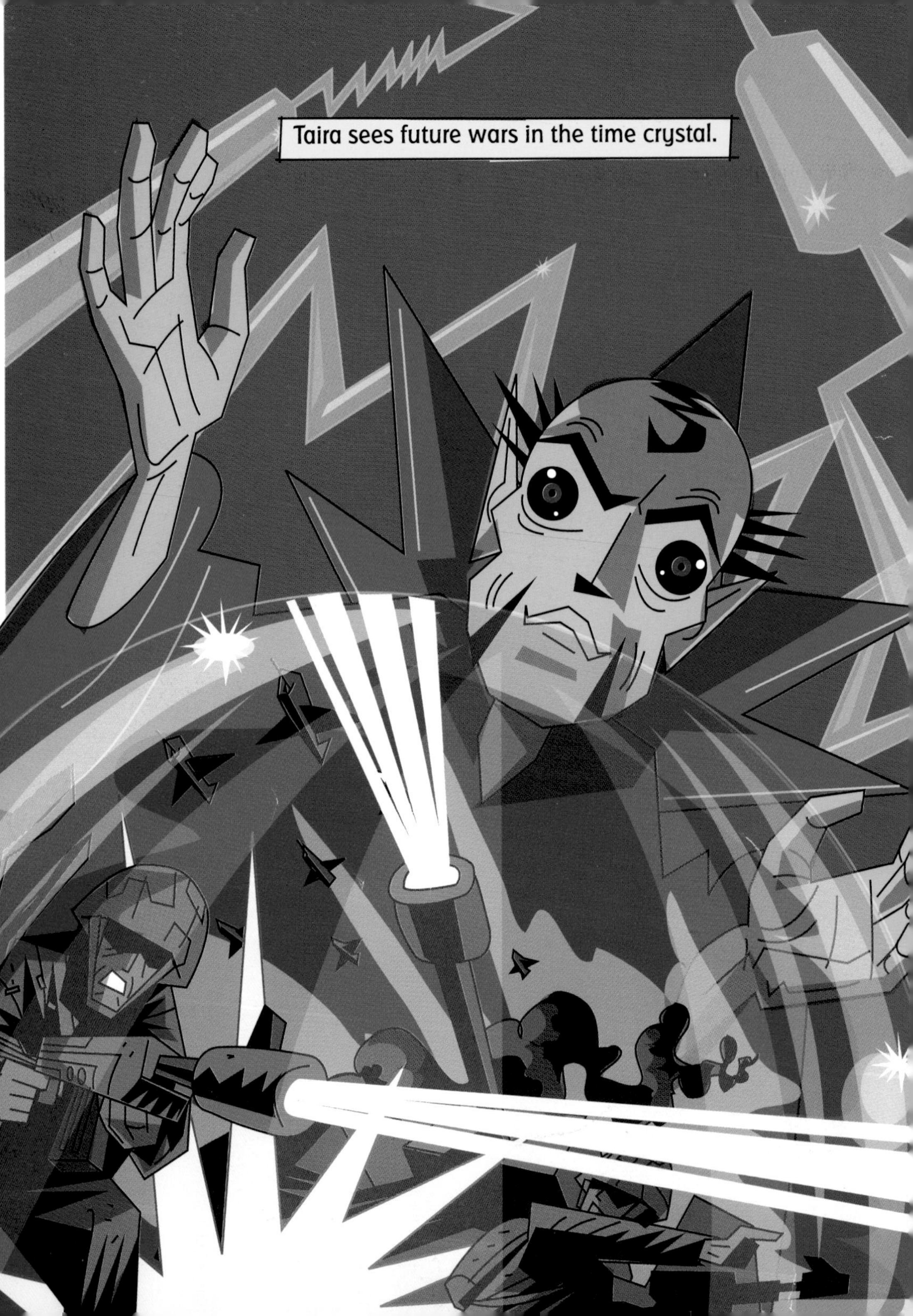
Taira sees future wars in the time crystal.

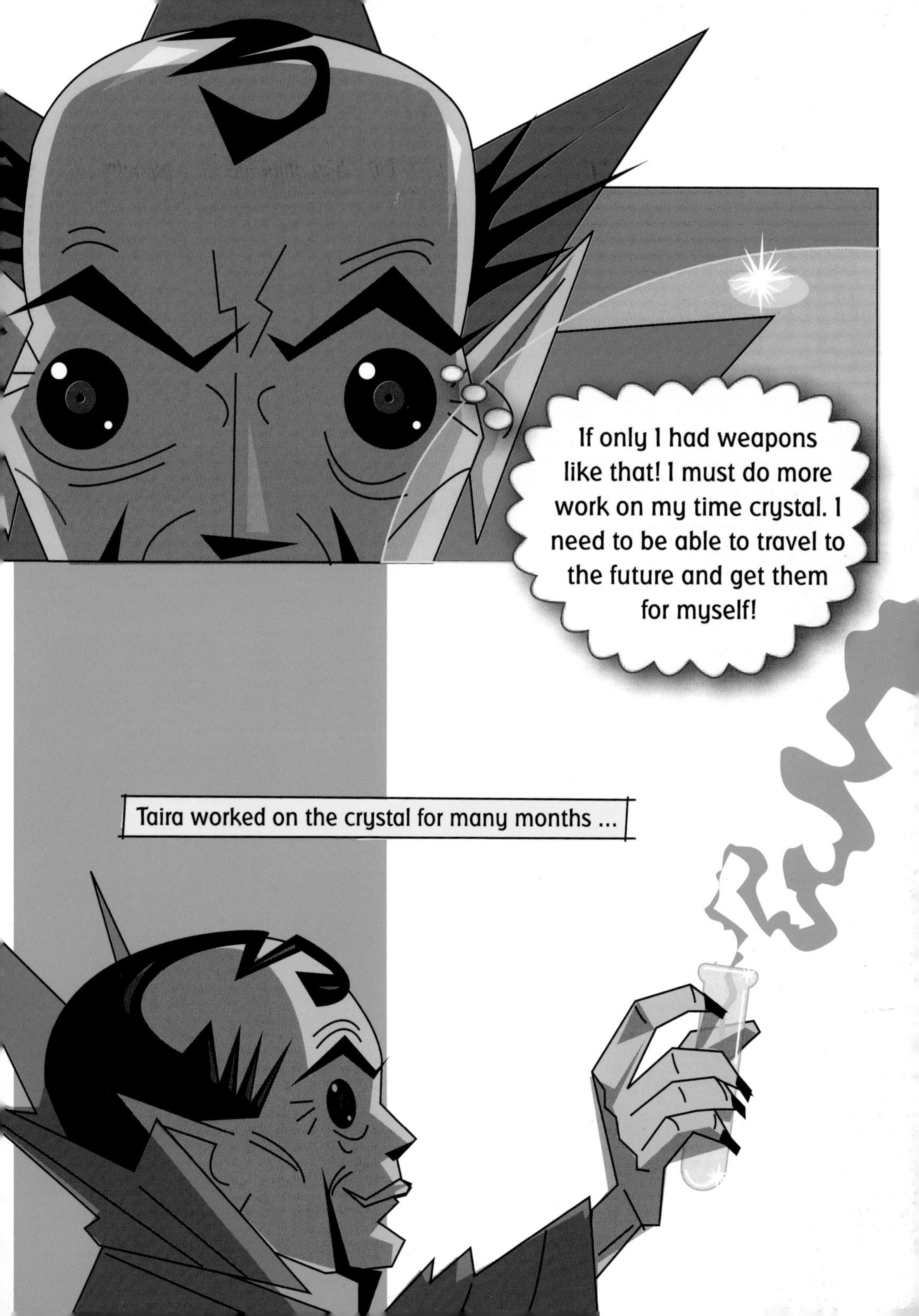
If only I had weapons like that! I must do more work on my time crystal. I need to be able to travel to the future and get them for myself!
Taira worked on the crystal for many months ...

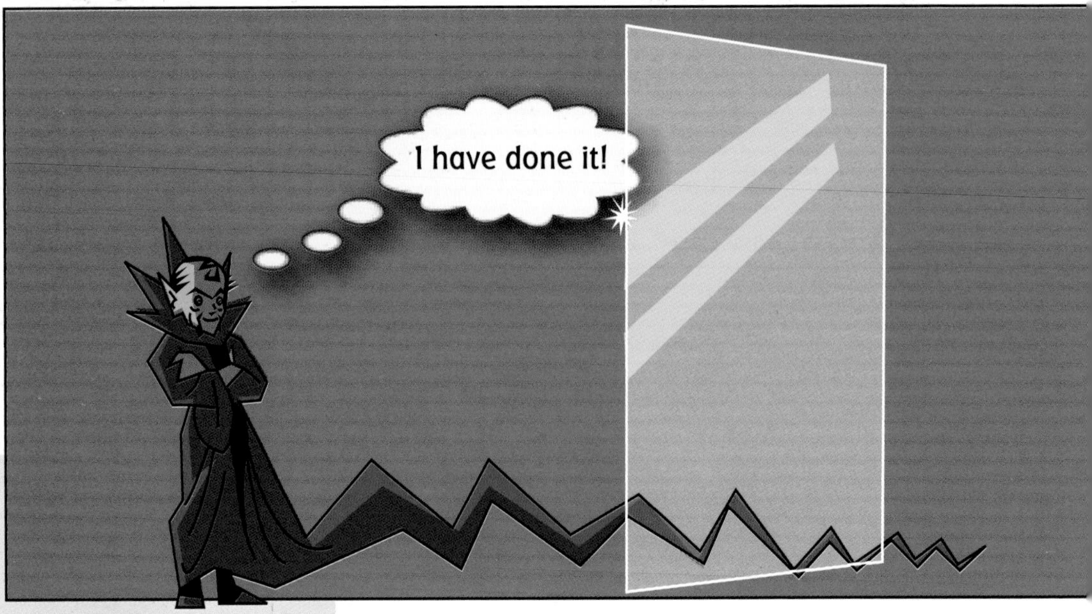
I have done it!

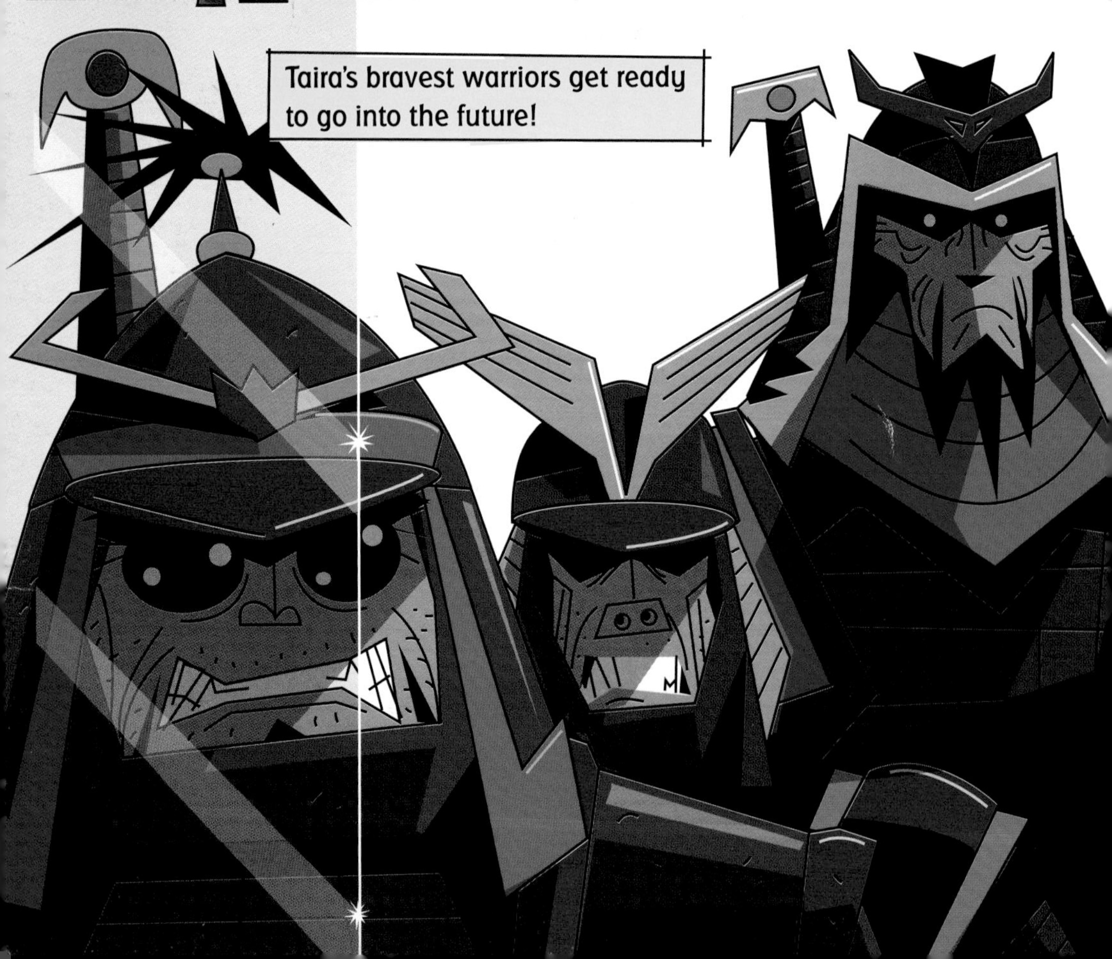
Taira's bravest warriors get ready to go into the future!

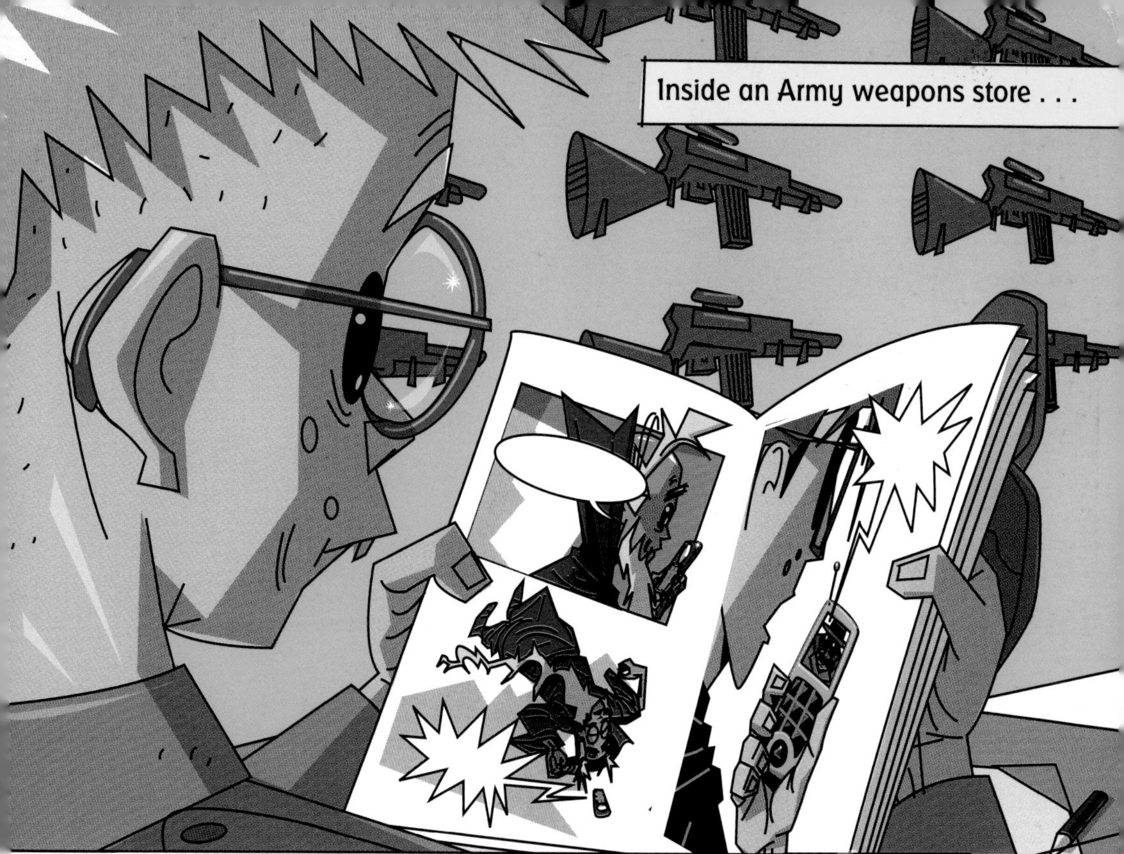
Inside an Army weapons store . . .

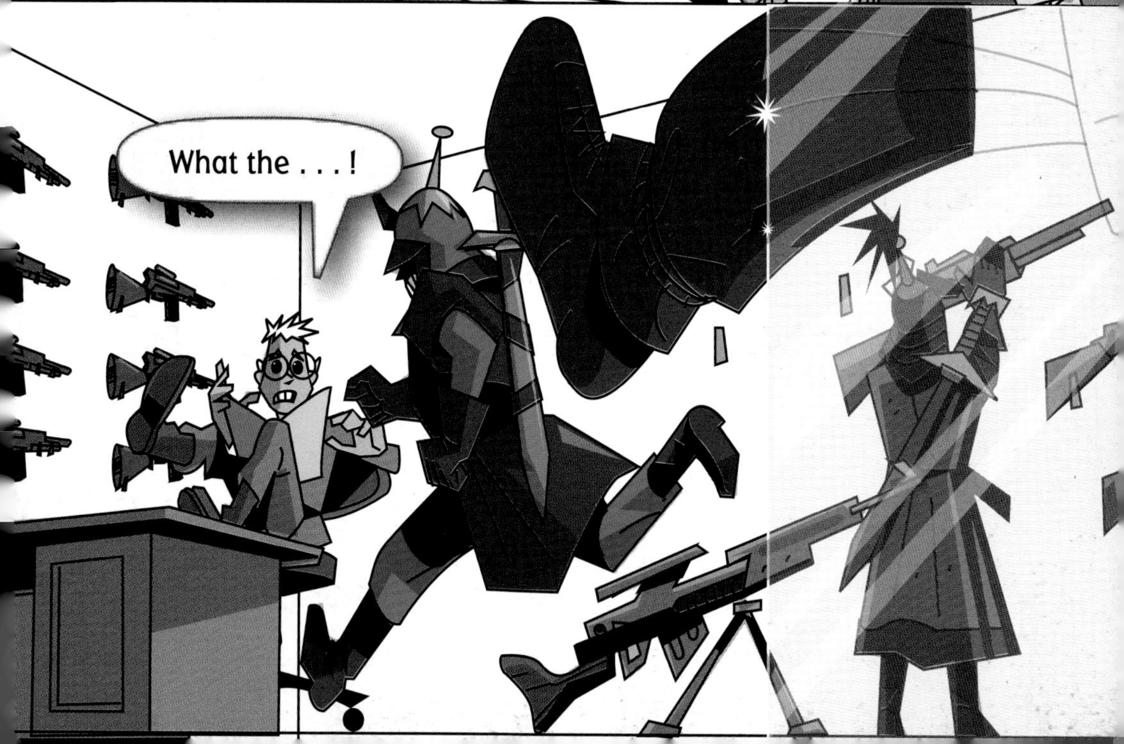
What the . . . !

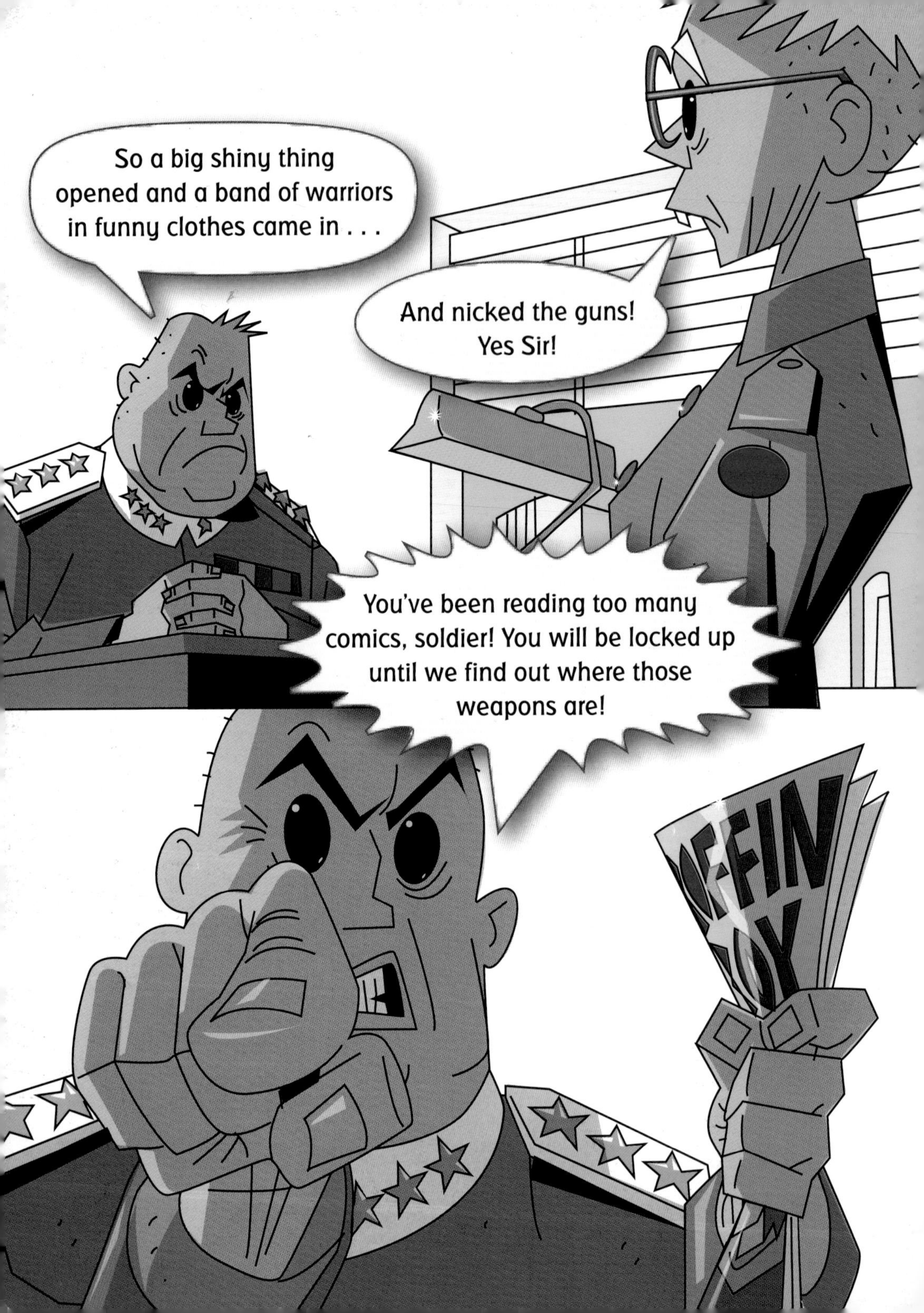
So a big shiny thing opened and a band of warriors in funny clothes came in . . .
And nicked the guns! Yes Sir!
You've been reading too many comics, soldier! You will be locked up until we find out where those weapons are!

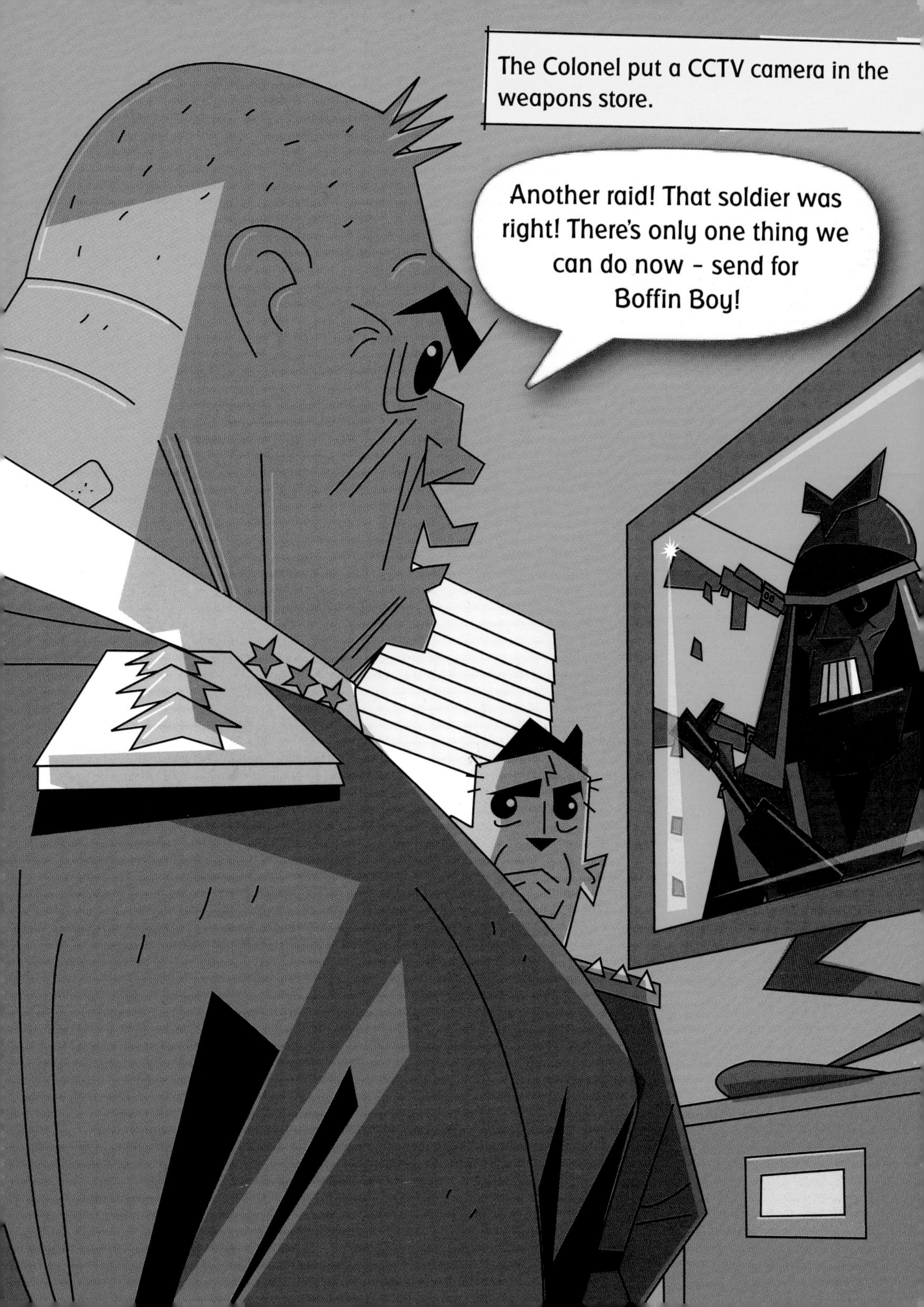
The Colonel put a CCTV camera in the weapons store.
Another raid! That soldier was right! There's only one thing we can do now - send for Boffin Boy!

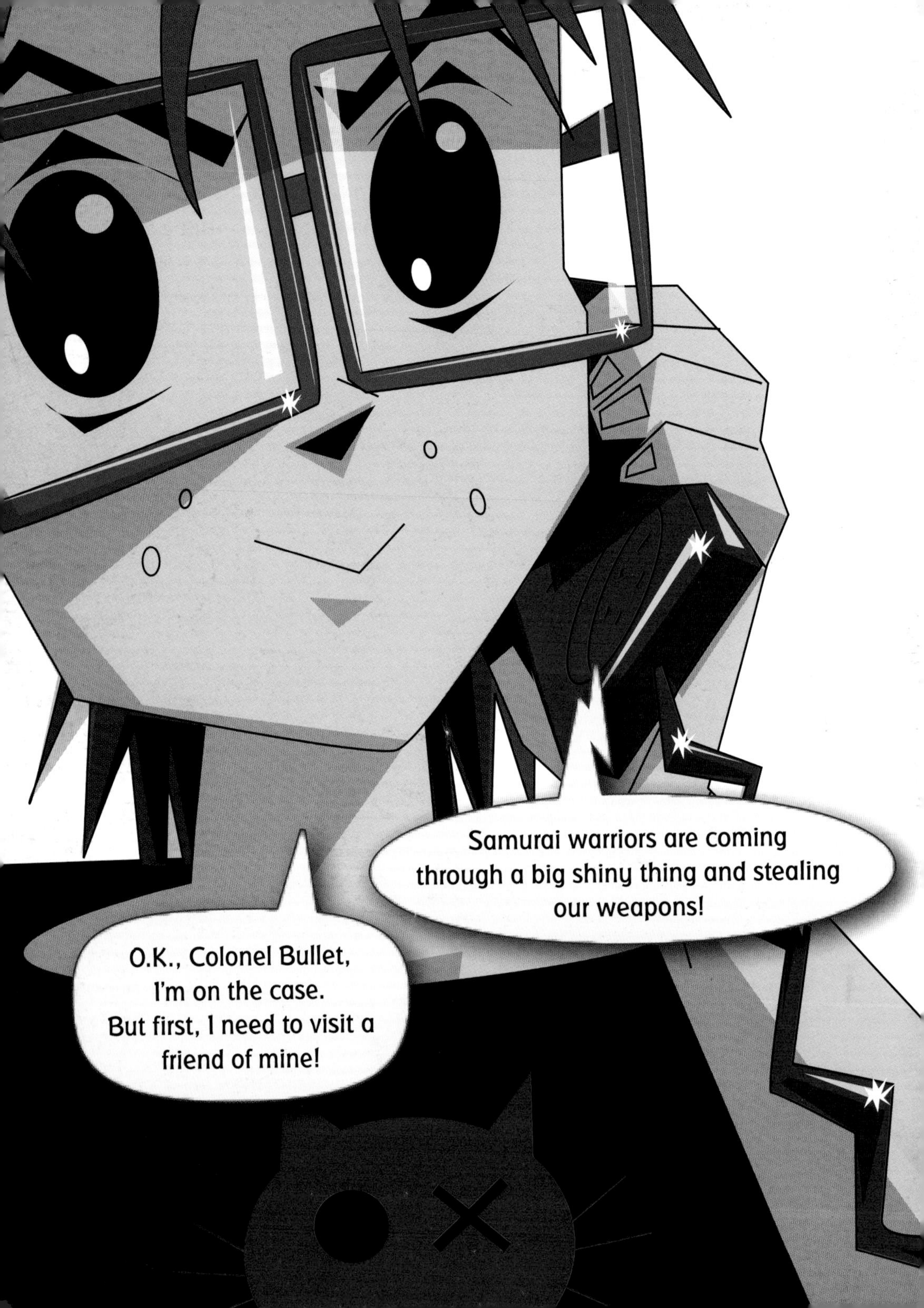
Samurai warriors are coming through a big shiny thing and stealing our weapons!
O.K., Colonel Bullet, I'm on the case. But first, I need to visit a friend of mine!

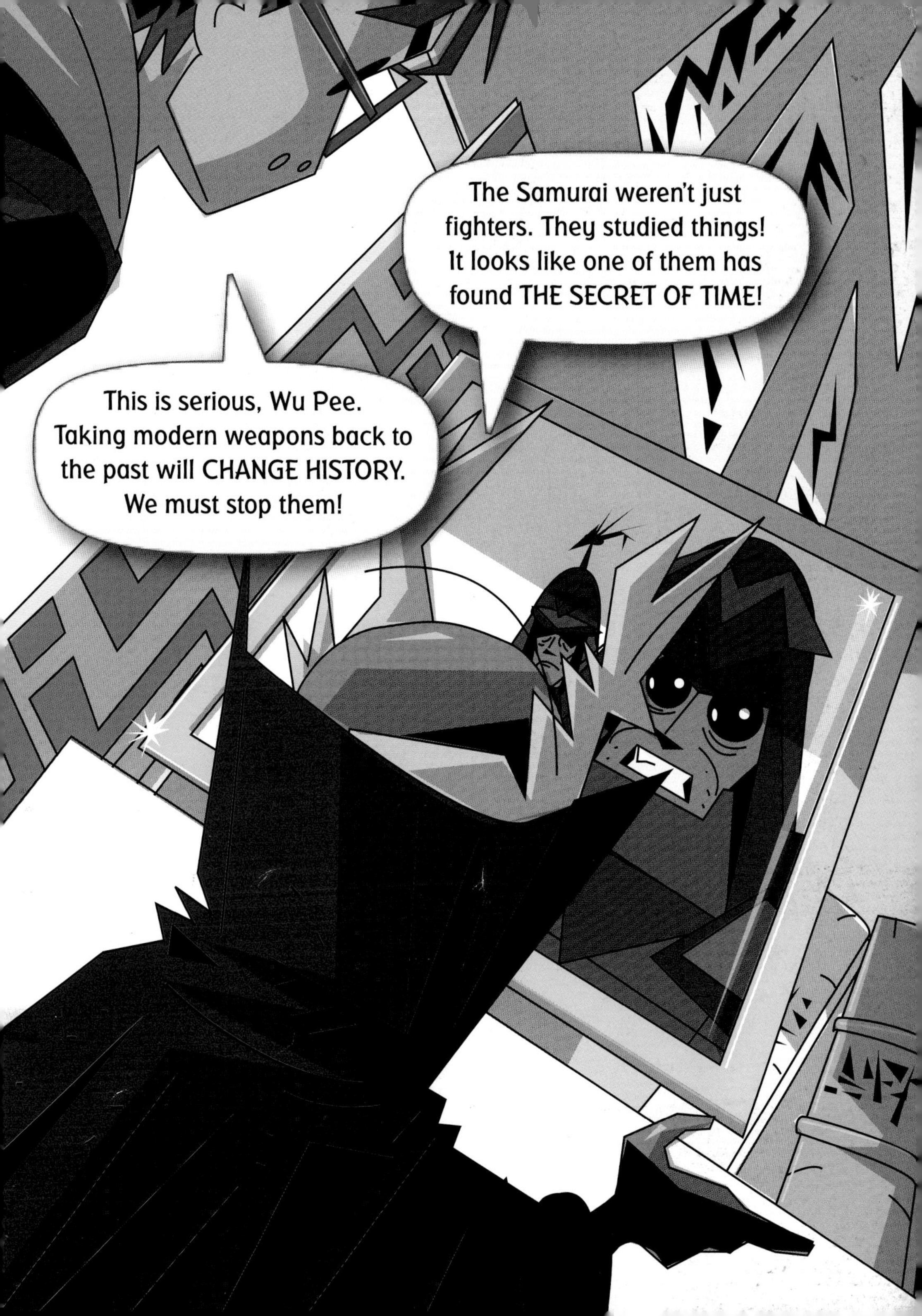
The Samurai weren't just fighters. They studied things! It looks like one of them has found THE SECRET OF TIME!
This is serious, Wu Pee. Taking modern weapons back to the past will CHANGE HISTORY. We must stop them!

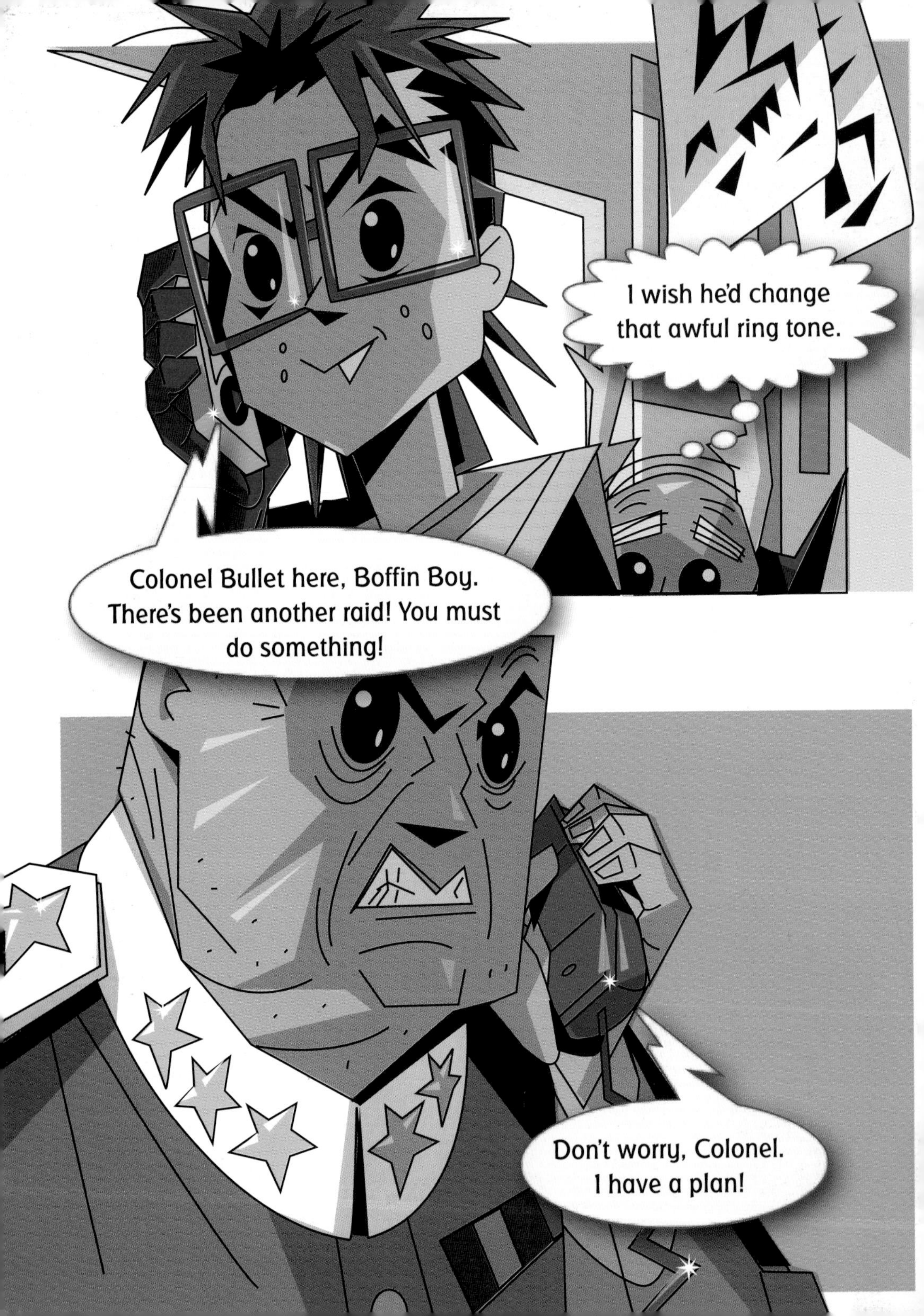
I wish he'd change that awful ring tone.
Colonel Bullet here, Boffin Boy. There's been another raid! You must do something!
Don't worry, Colonel. I have a plan!

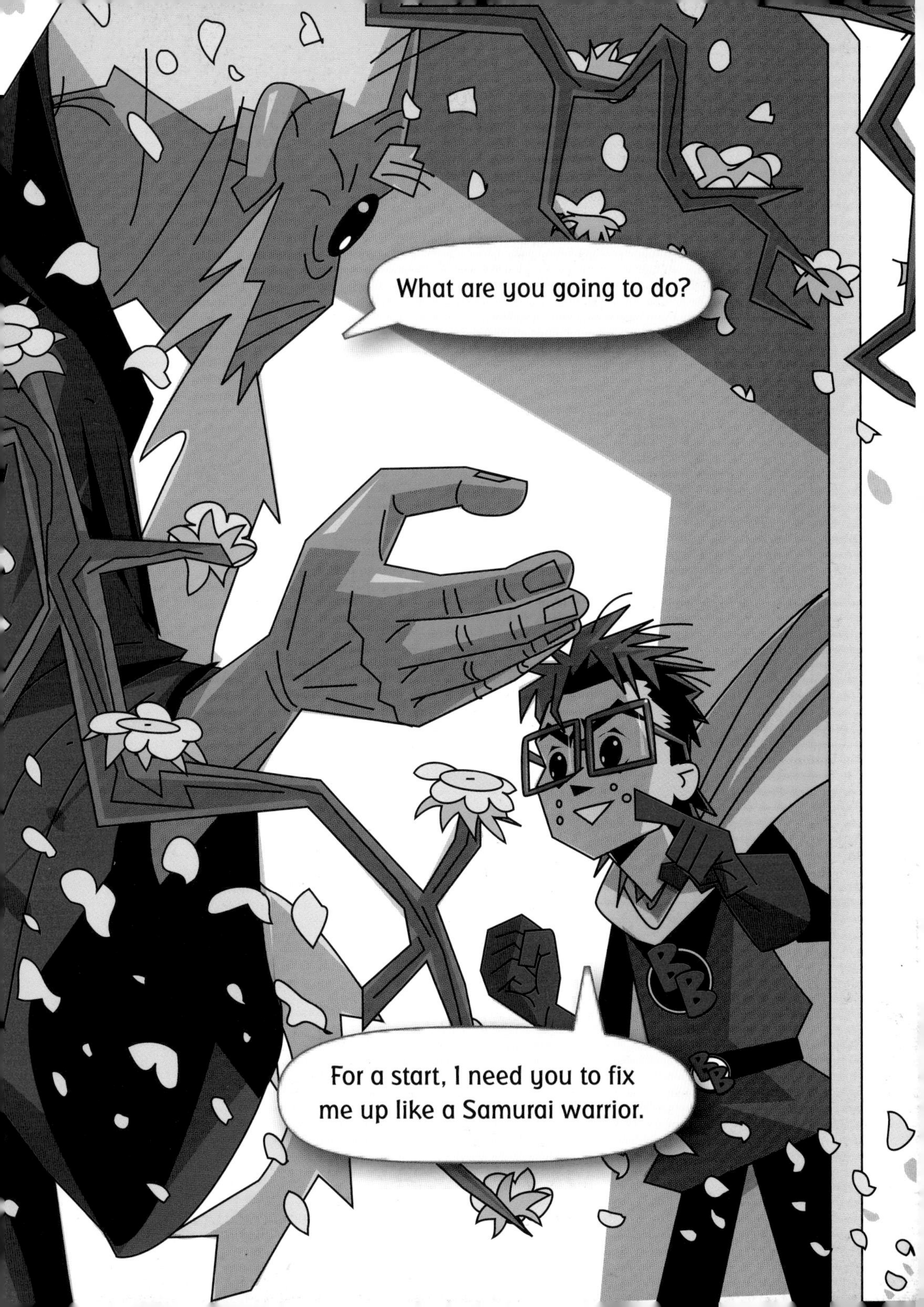
What are you going to do?
For a start, I need you to fix me up like a Samurai warrior.

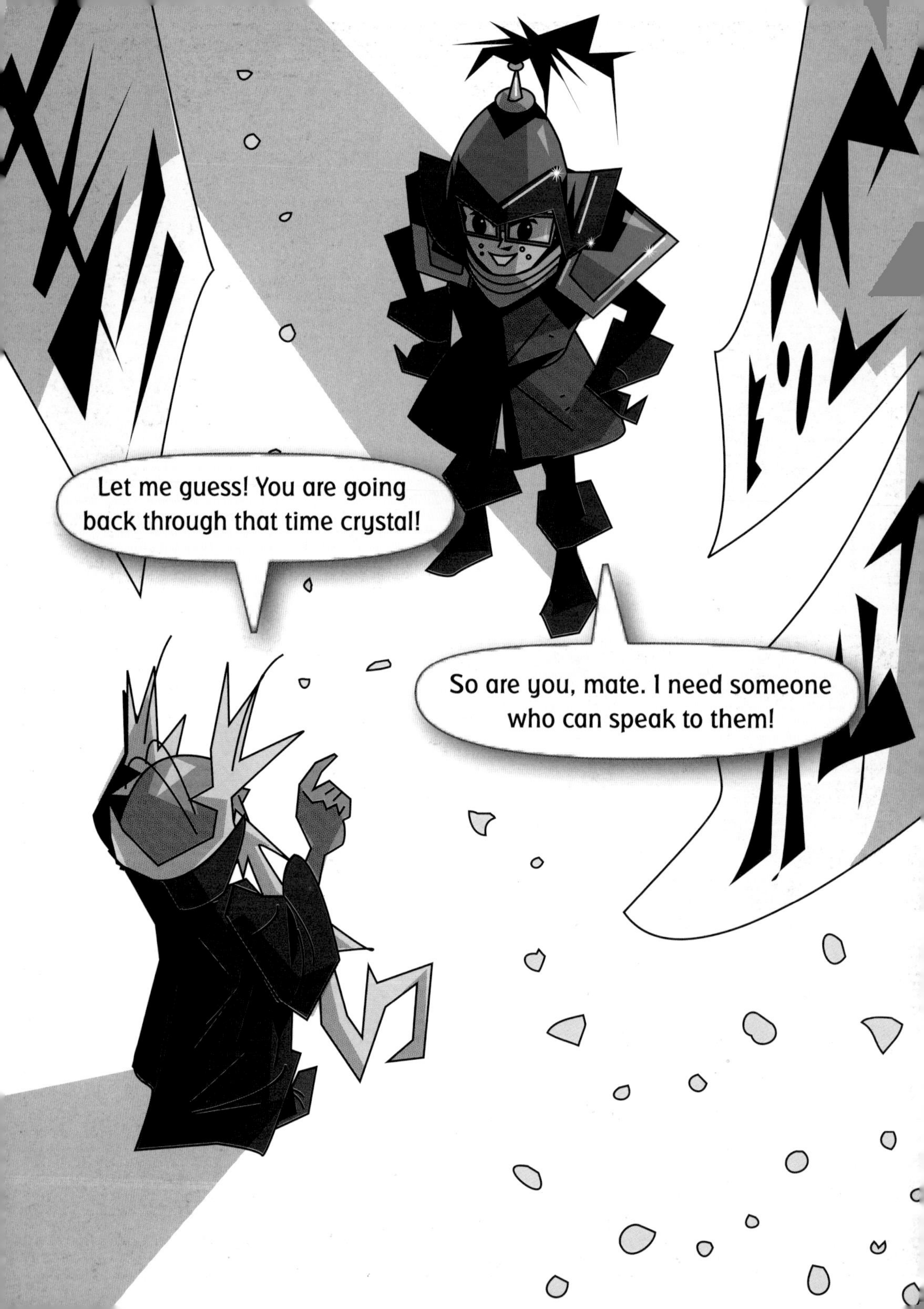
Let me guess! You are going back through that time crystal!
So are you, mate. I need someone who can speak to them!

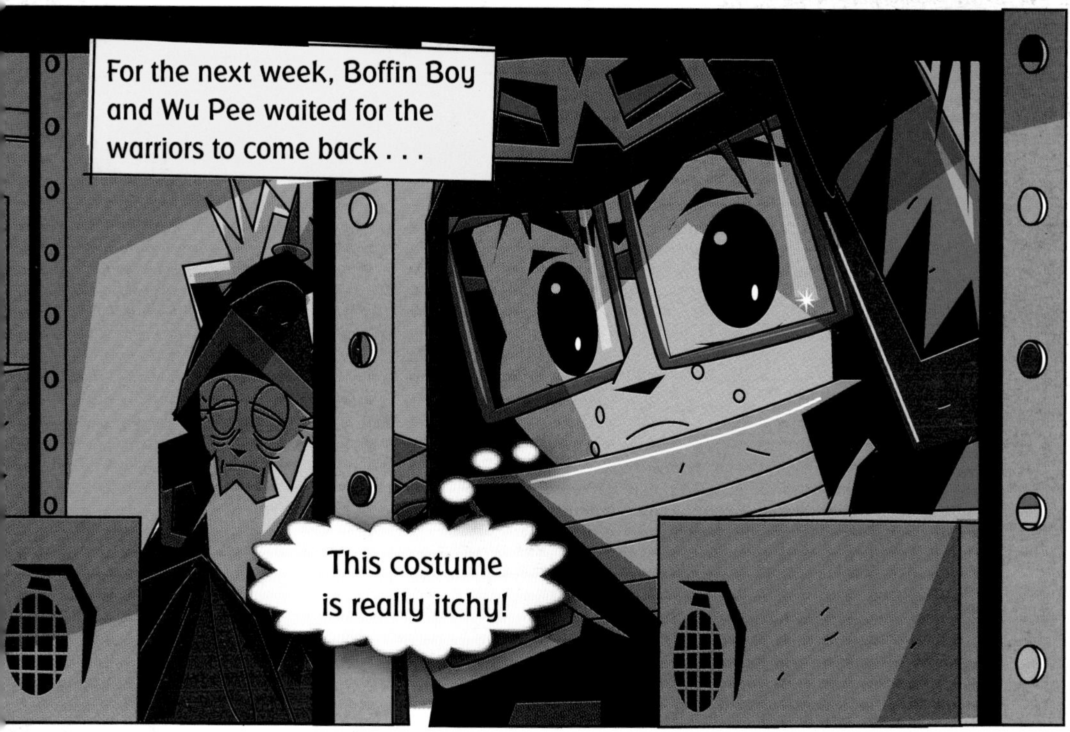
For the next week, Boffin Boy and Wu Pee waited for the warriors to come back . . .
This costume is really itchy!

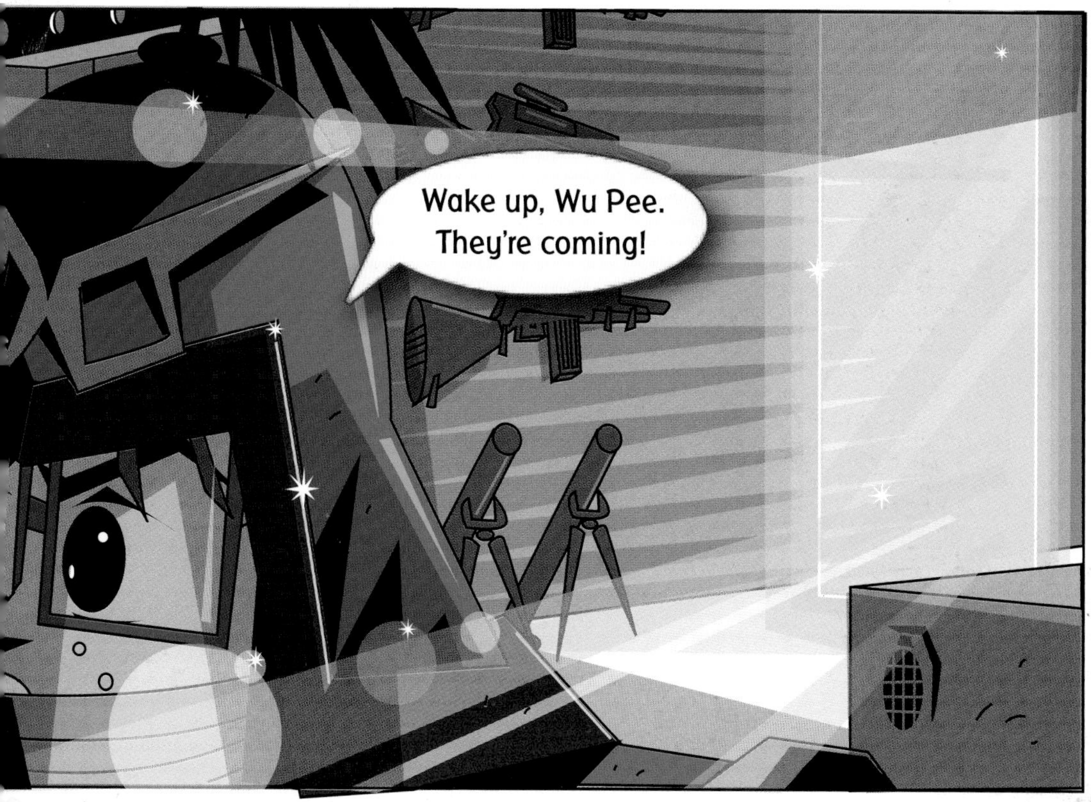
Wake up, Wu Pee. They're coming!

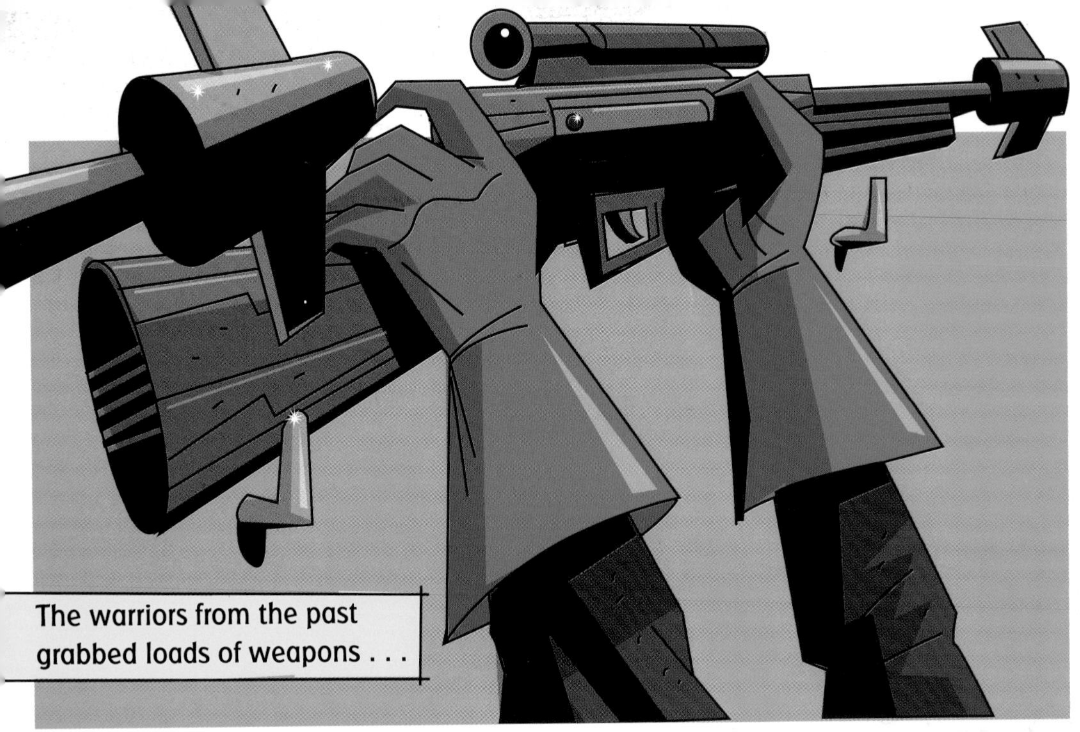
The warriors from the past grabbed loads of weapons . . .

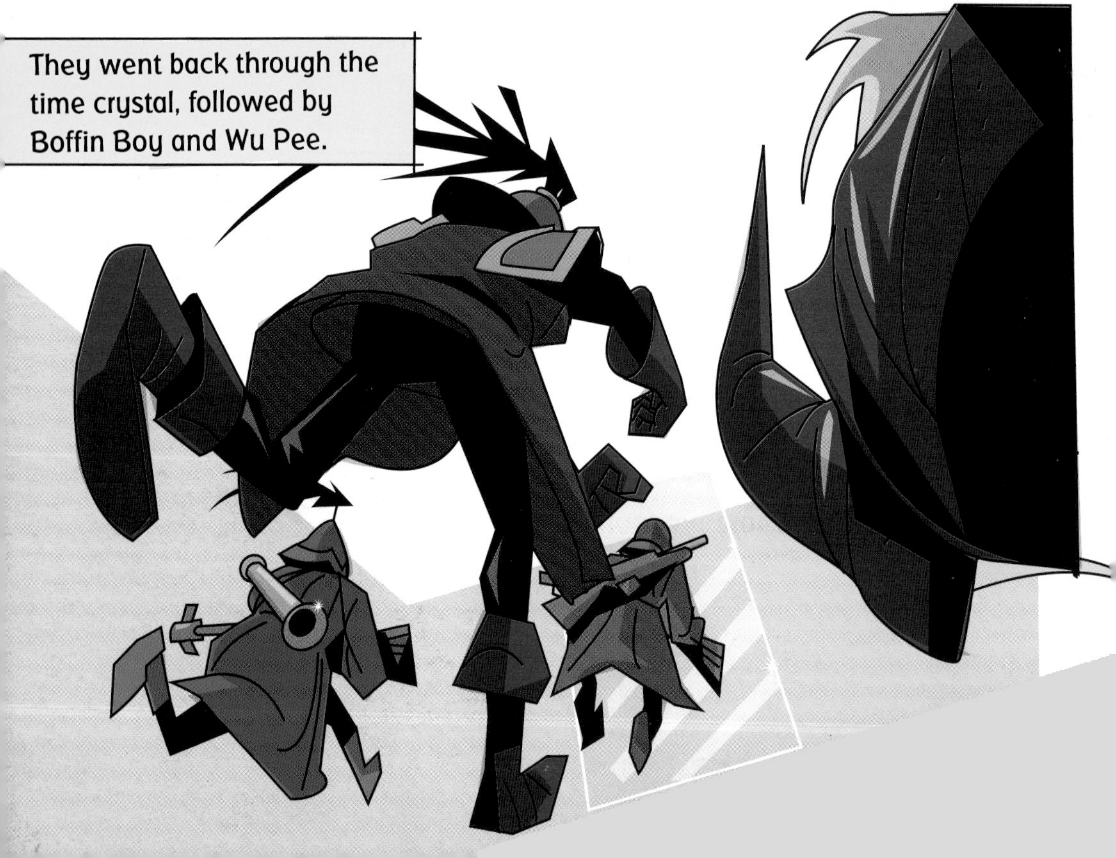
They went back through the time crystal, followed by Boffin Boy and Wu Pee.

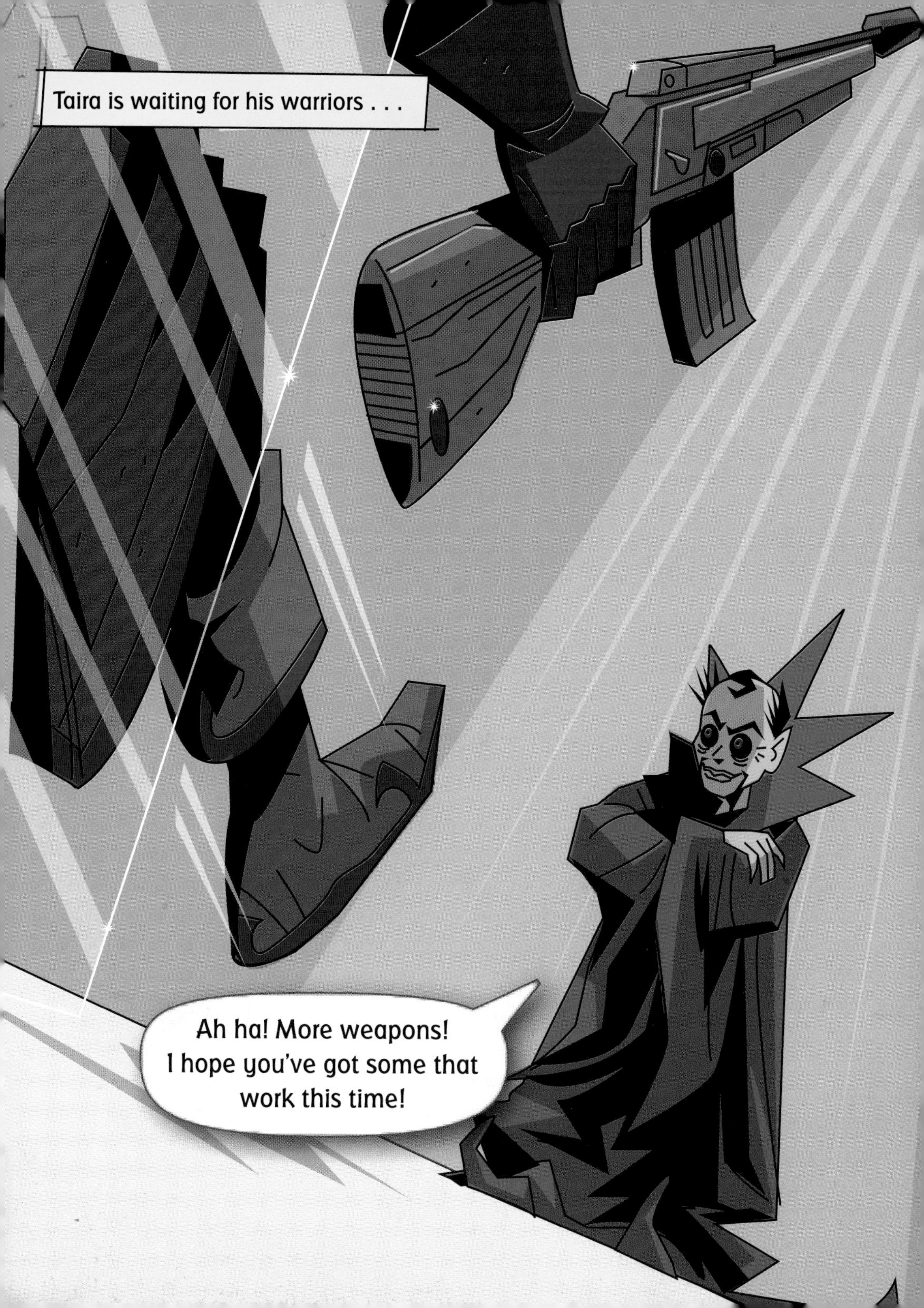
Taira is waiting for his warriors . . .
Ah ha! More weapons! I hope you've got some that work this time!

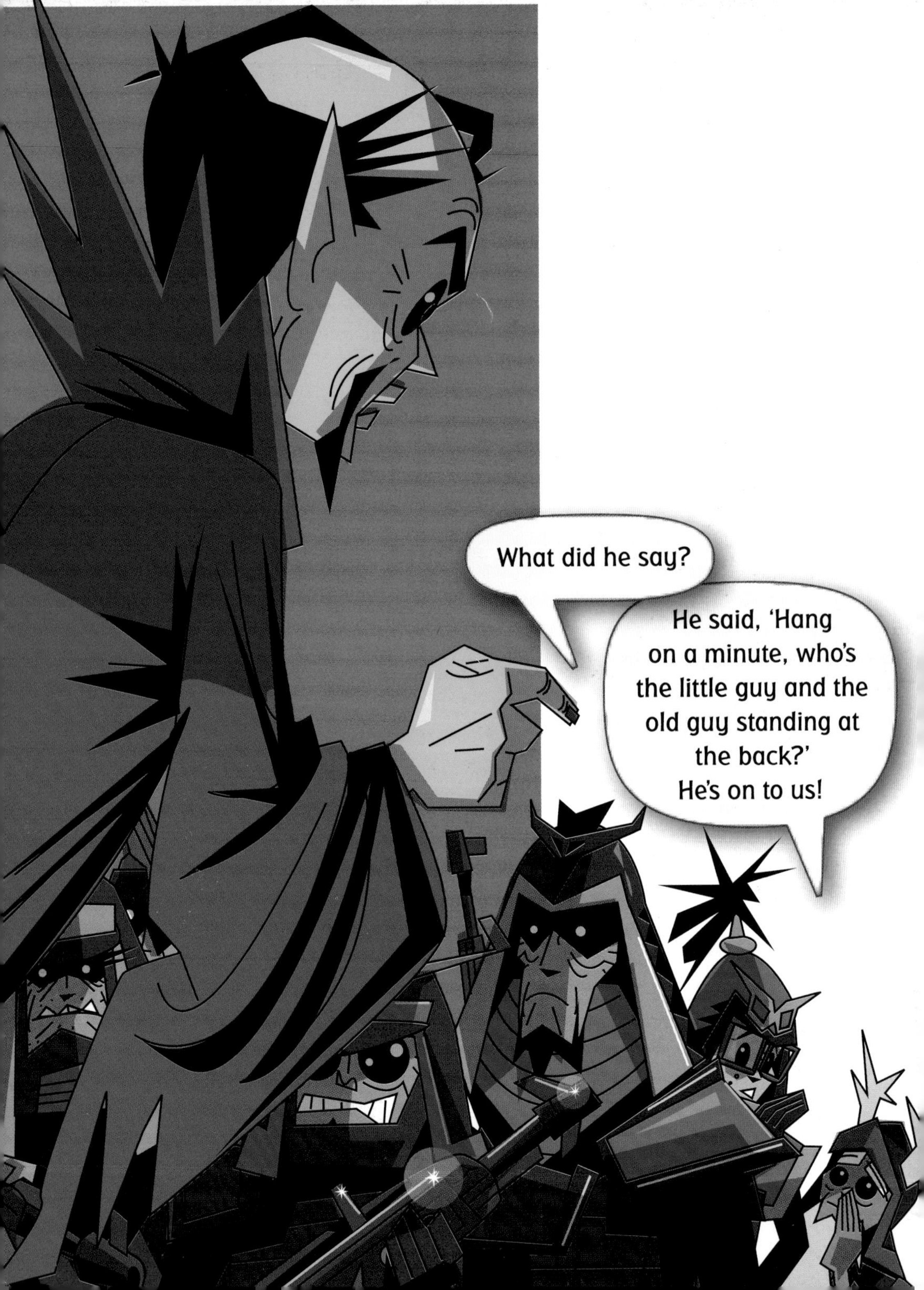
What did he say?
He said, 'Hang on a minute, who's the little guy and the old guy standing at the back?' He's on to us!

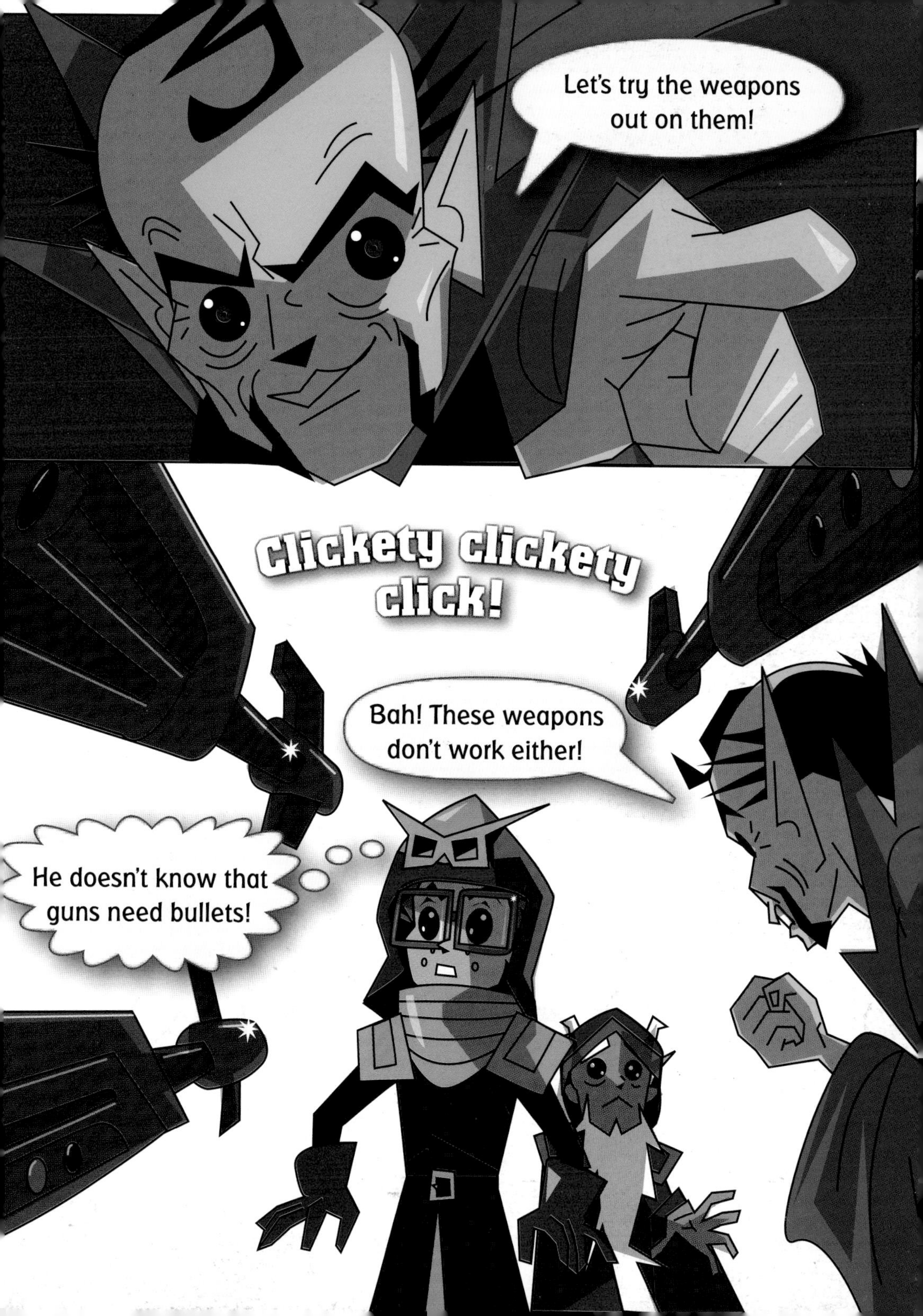
Let's try the weapons out on them!
Clickety clickety click!
Bah! These weapons don't work either!
He doesn't know that guns need bullets!

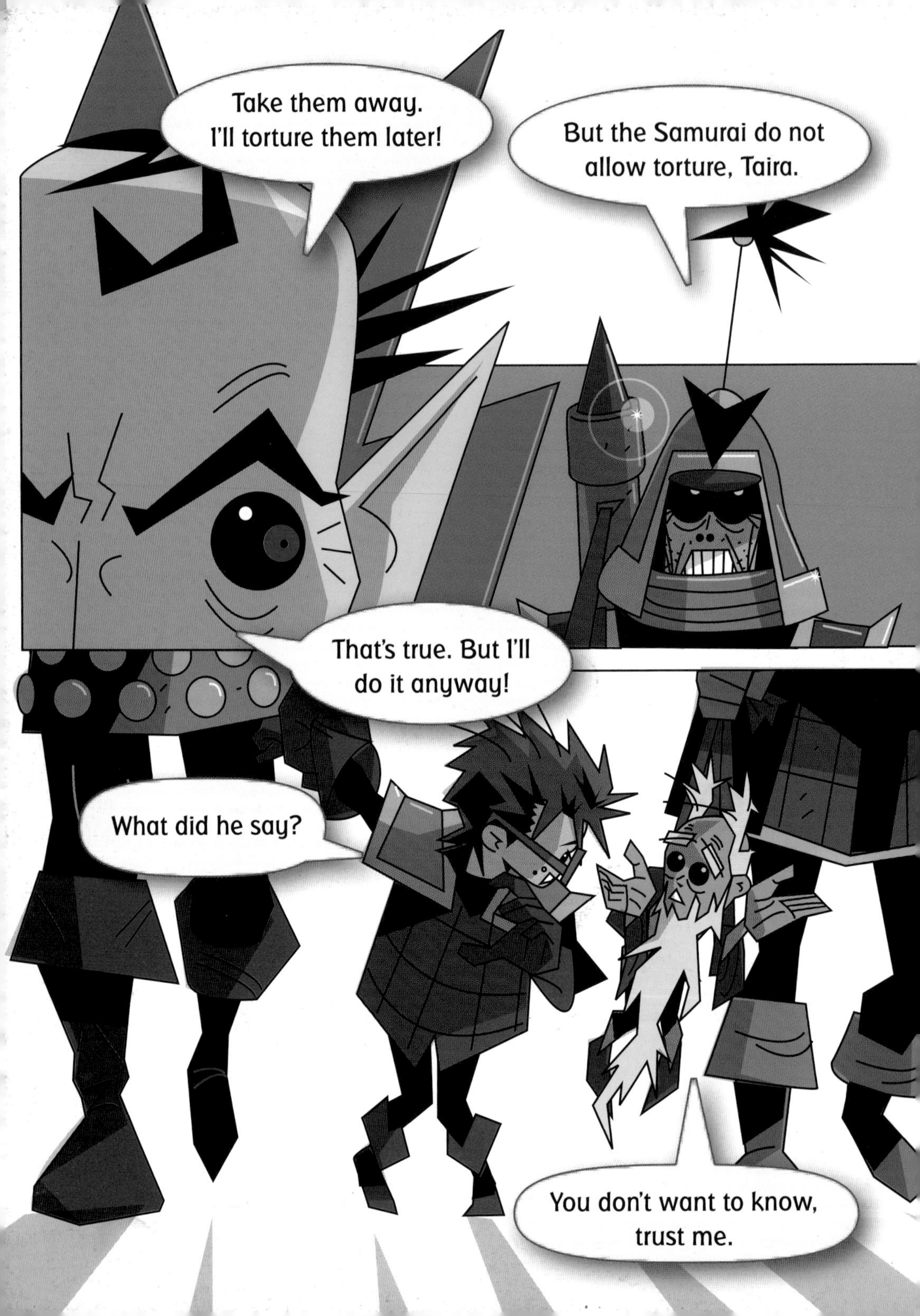
Take them away. I'll torture them later!
But the Samurai do not allow torture, Taira.
That's true. But I'll do it anyway!
What did he say?
You don't want to know, trust me.

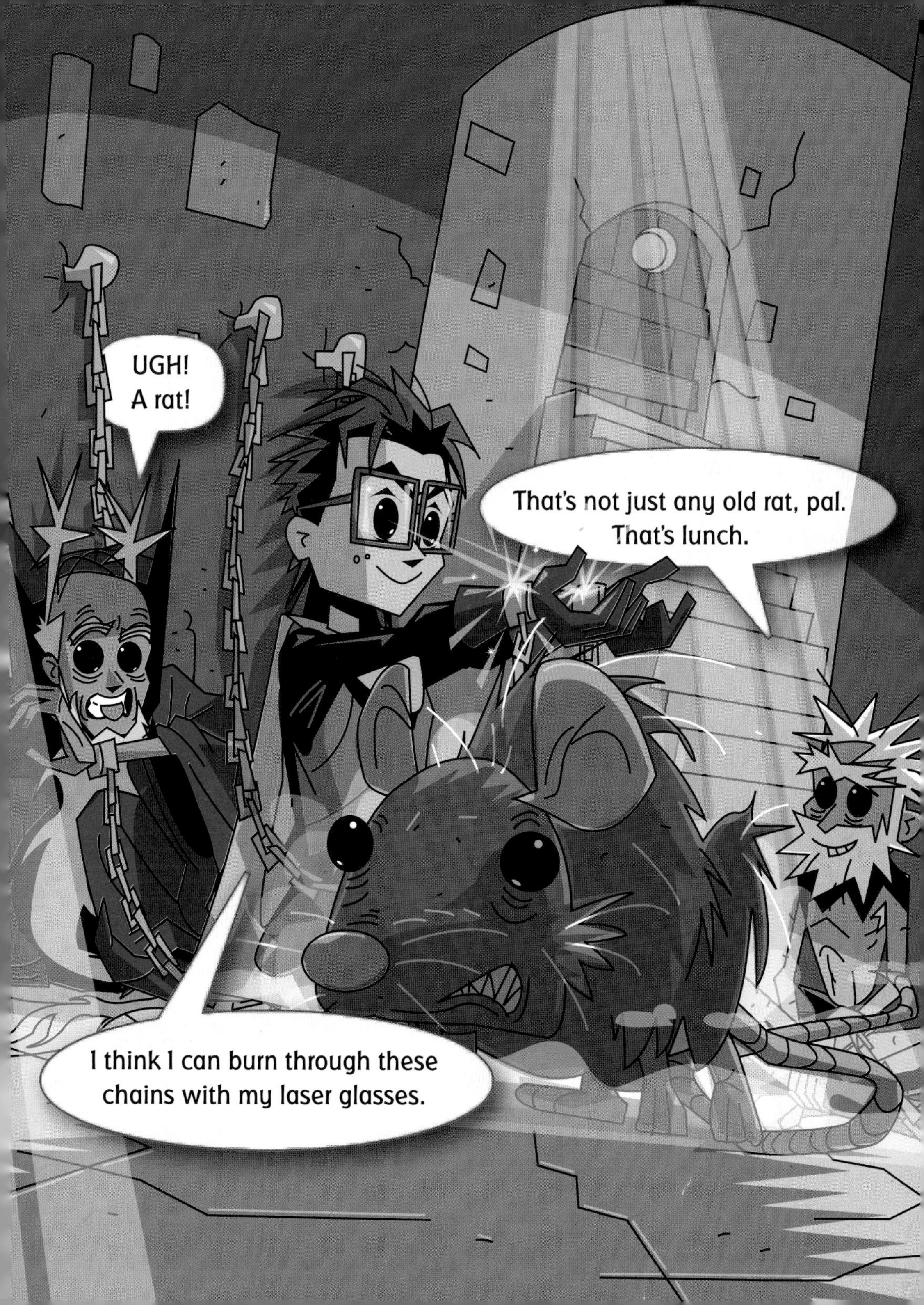
UGH! A rat!
That's not just any old rat, pal. That's lunch.
I think I can burn through these chains with my laser glasses.

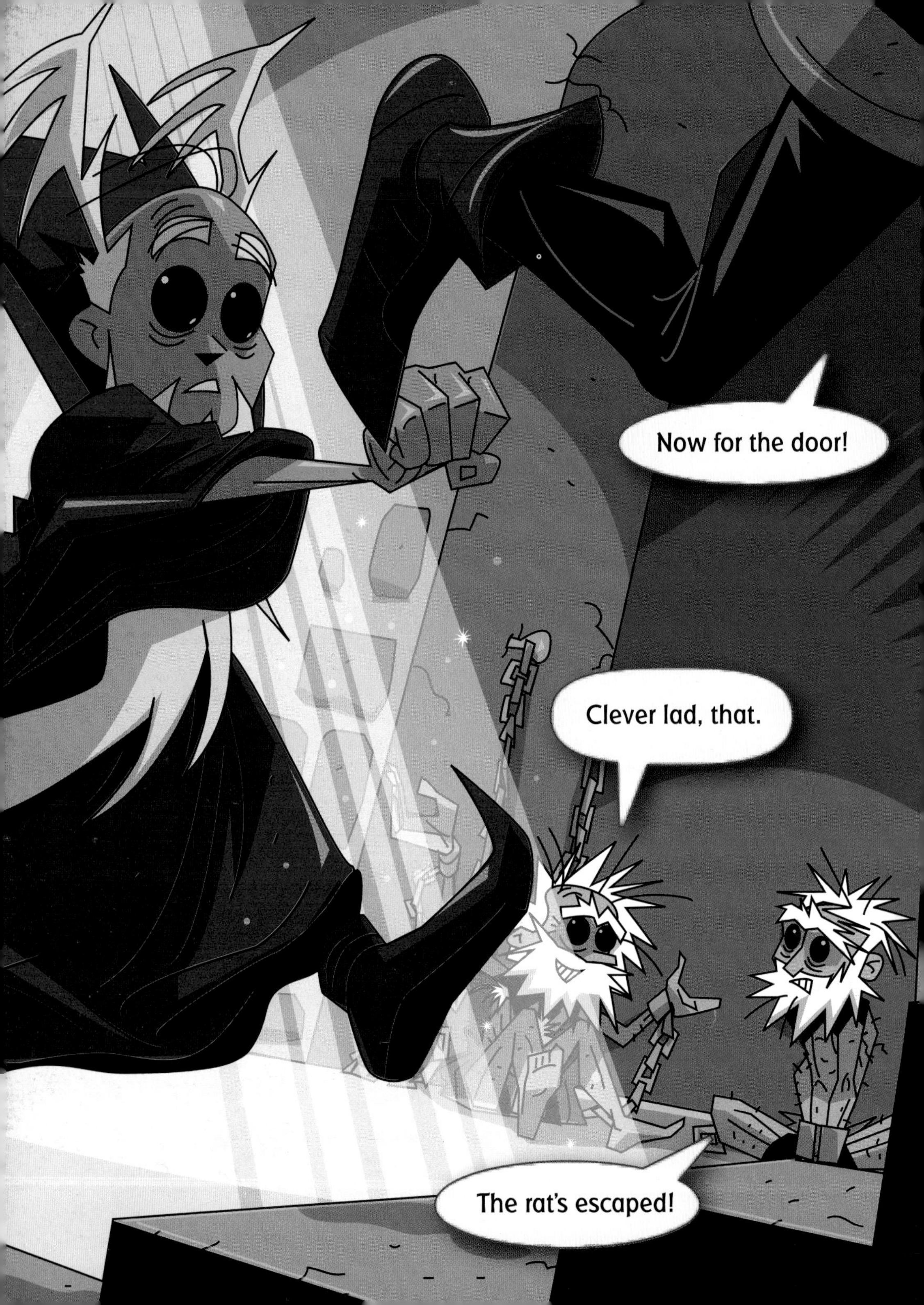
Now for the door!
Clever lad, that.
The rat's escaped!

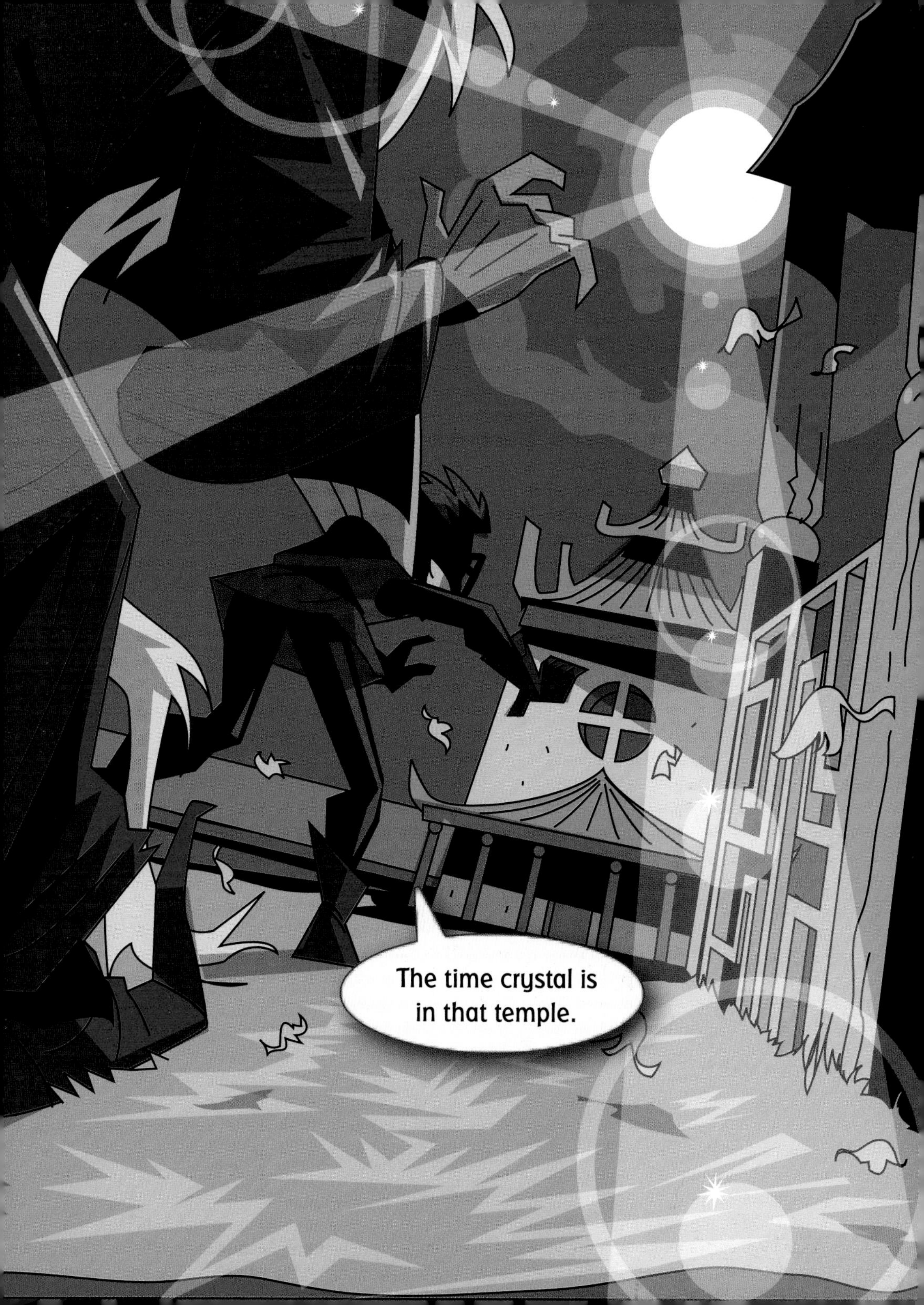
The time crystal is in that temple.

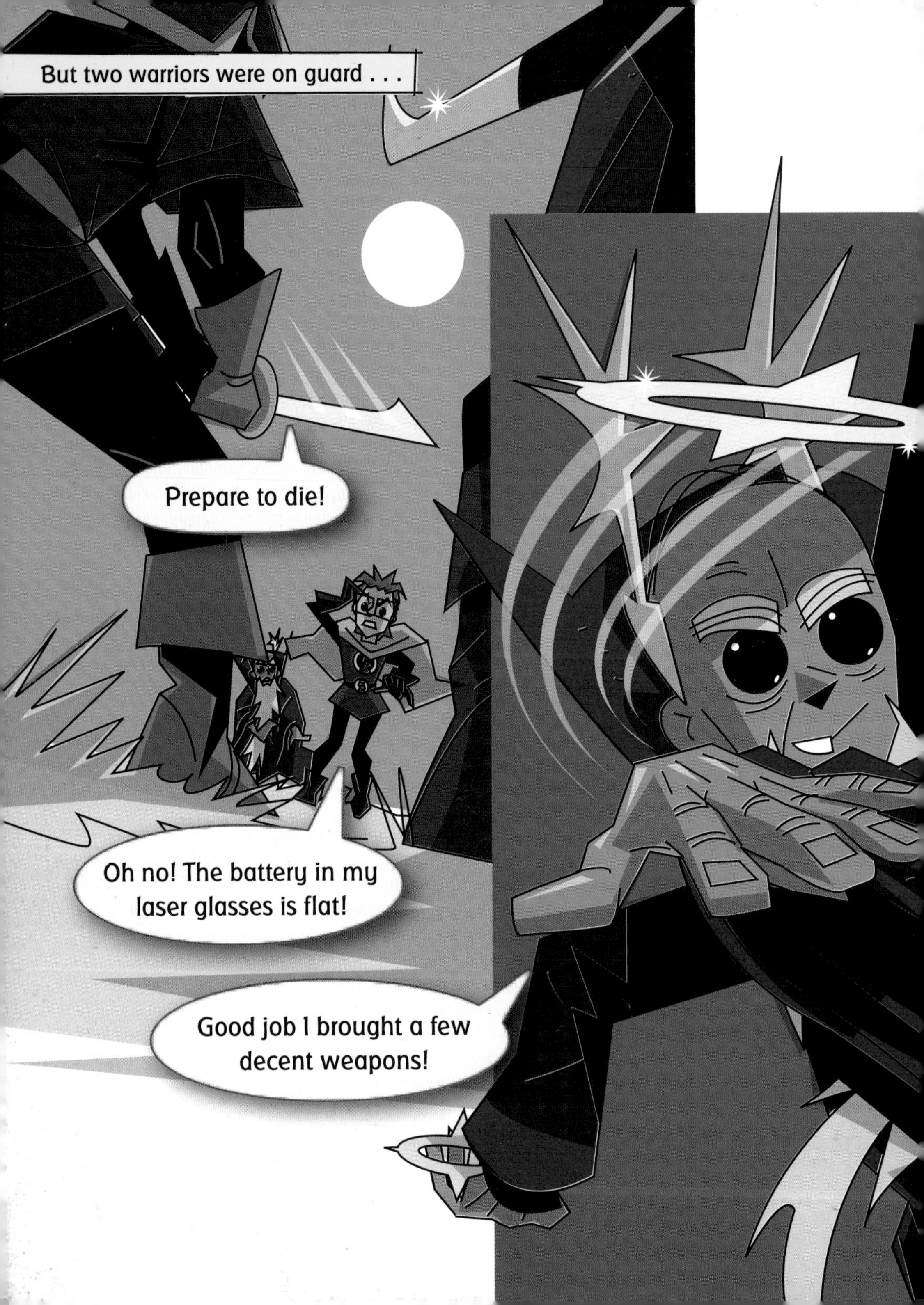
But two warriors were on guard . . .
Prepare to die!
Oh no! The battery in my laser glasses is flat!
Good job I brought a few decent weapons!

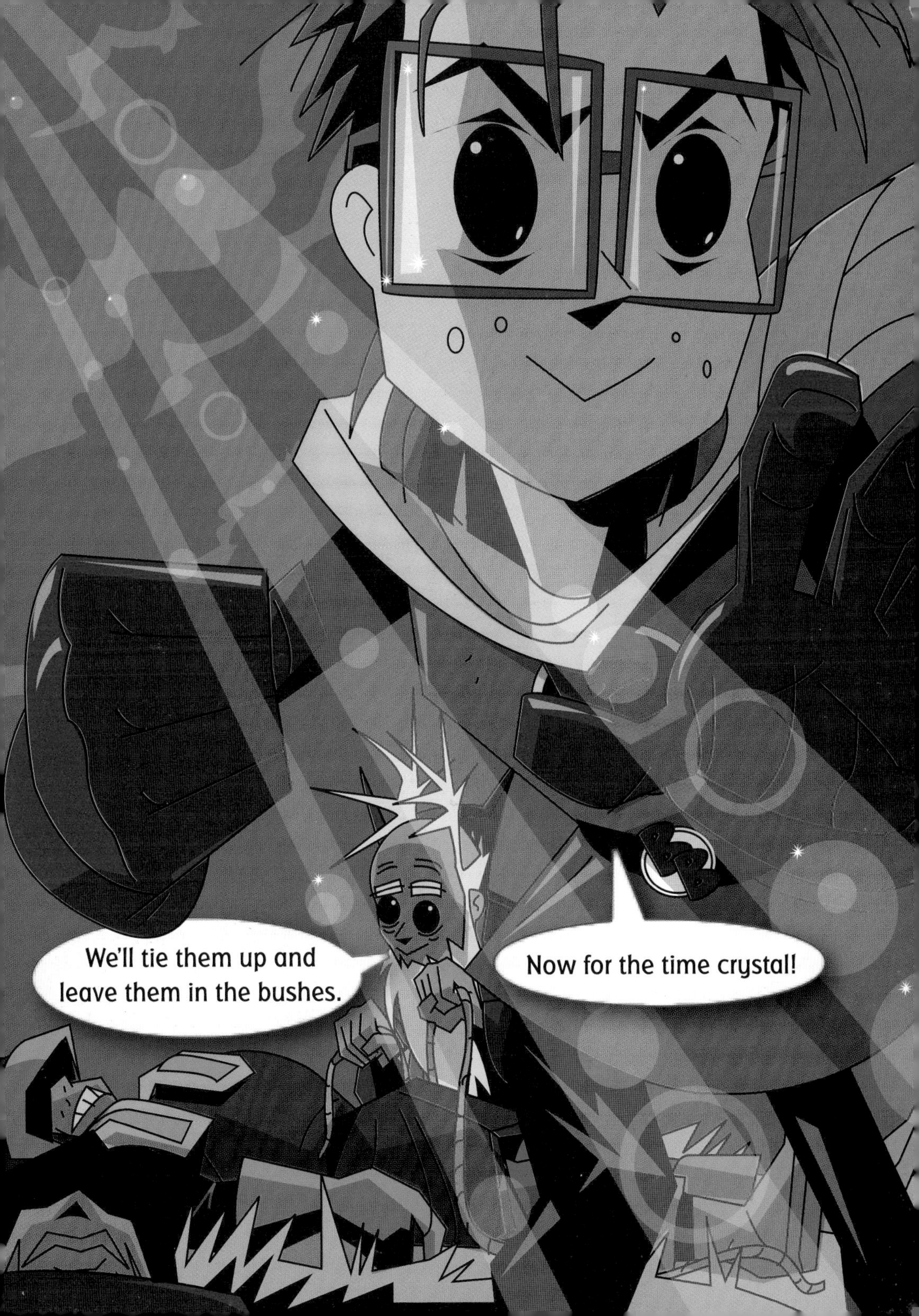
We'll tie them up and leave them in the bushes.
Now for the time crystal!

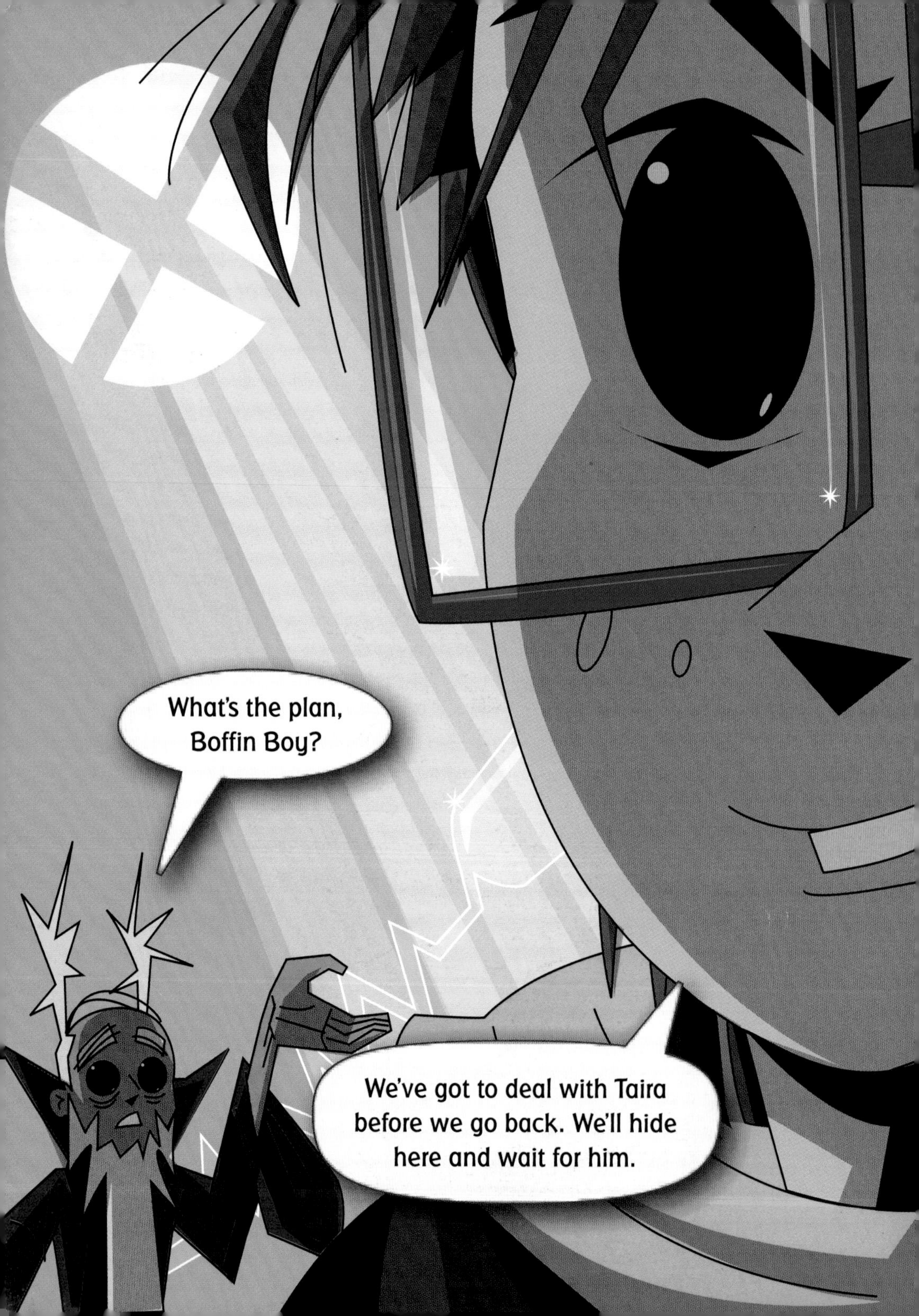
What's the plan, Boffin Boy?
We've got to deal with Taira before we go back. We'll hide here and wait for him.

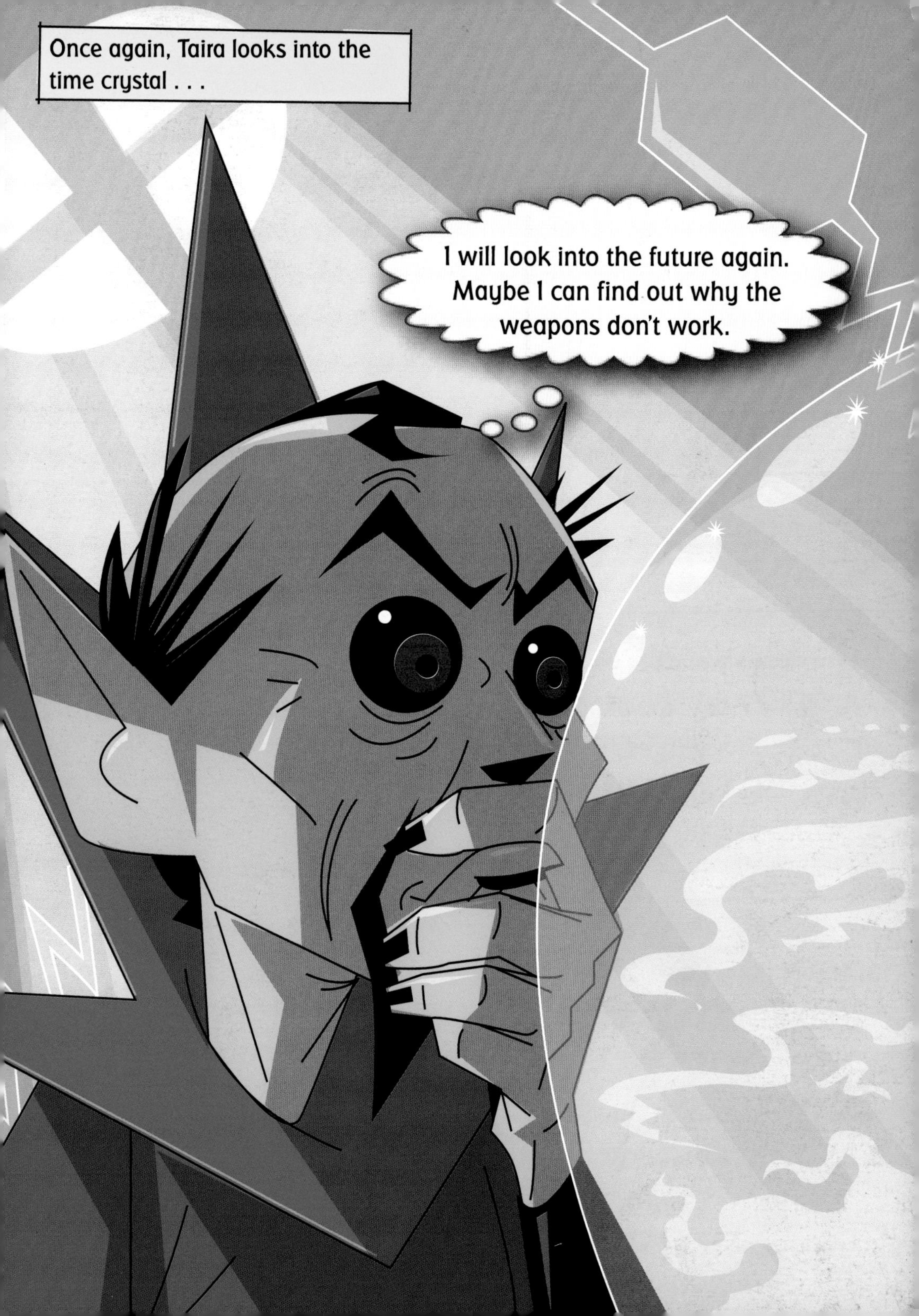
Once again, Taira looks into the time crystal . . .
I will look into the future again. Maybe I can find out why the weapons don't work.

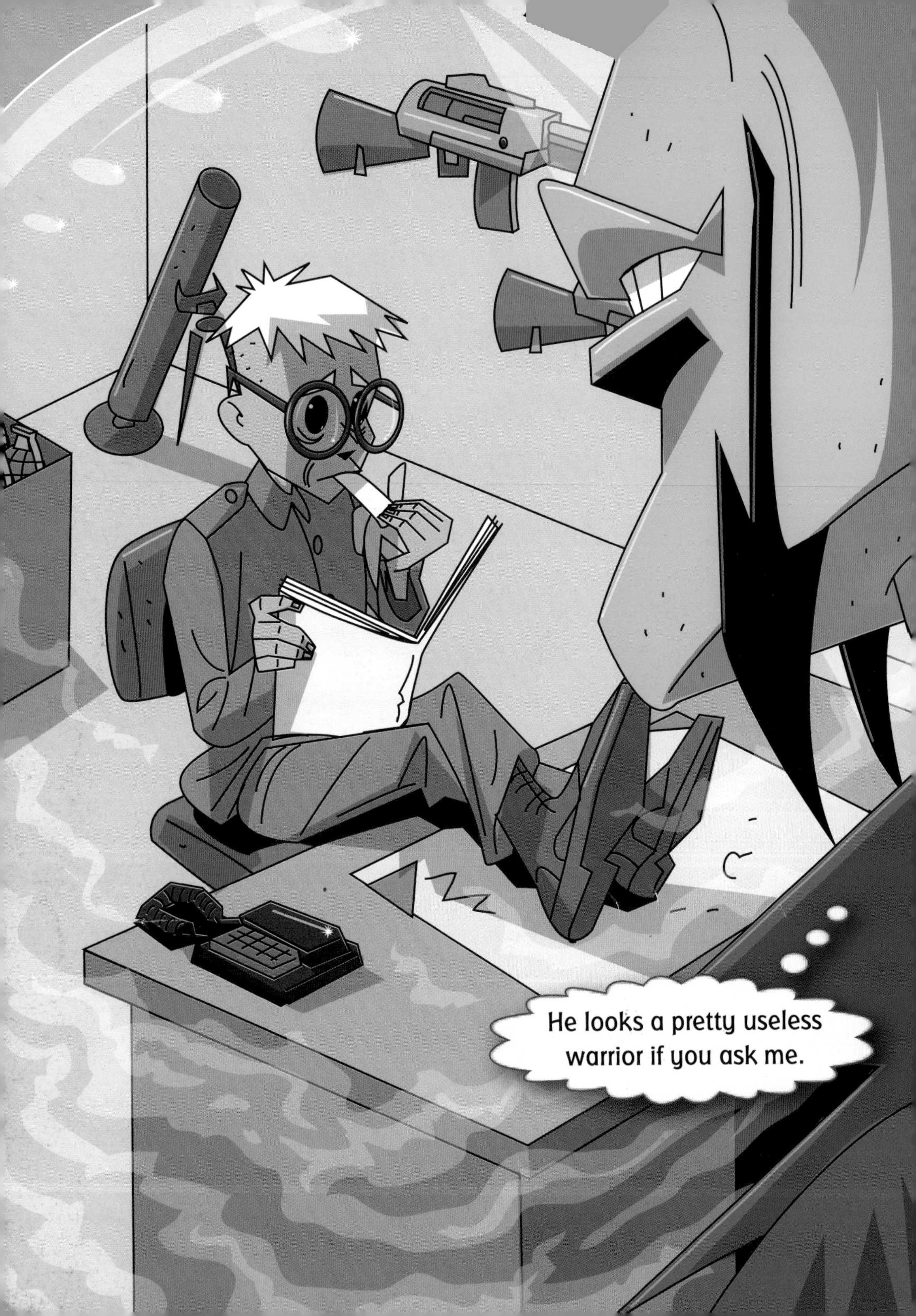
He looks a pretty useless warrior if you ask me.

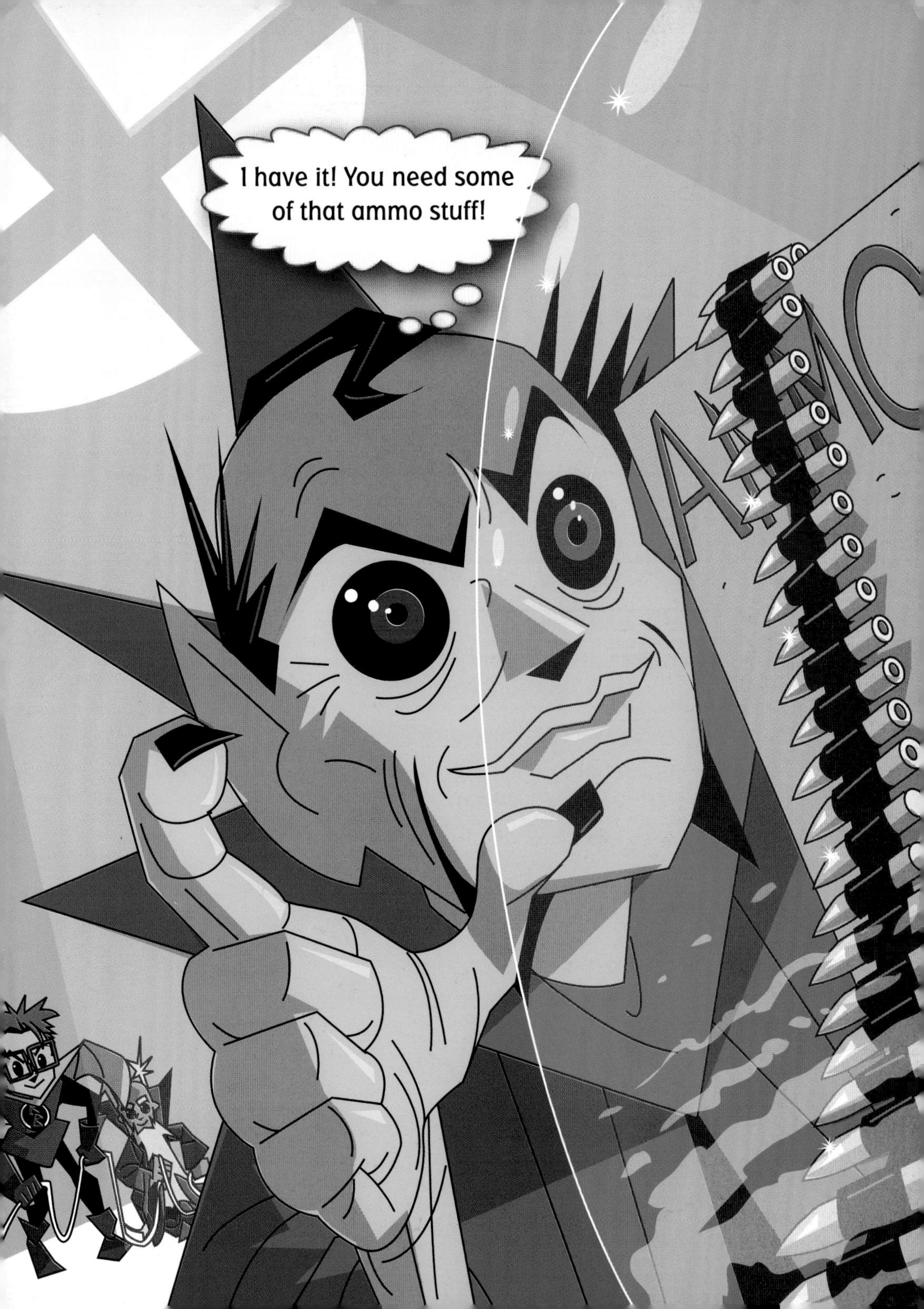
I have it! You need some of that ammo stuff!

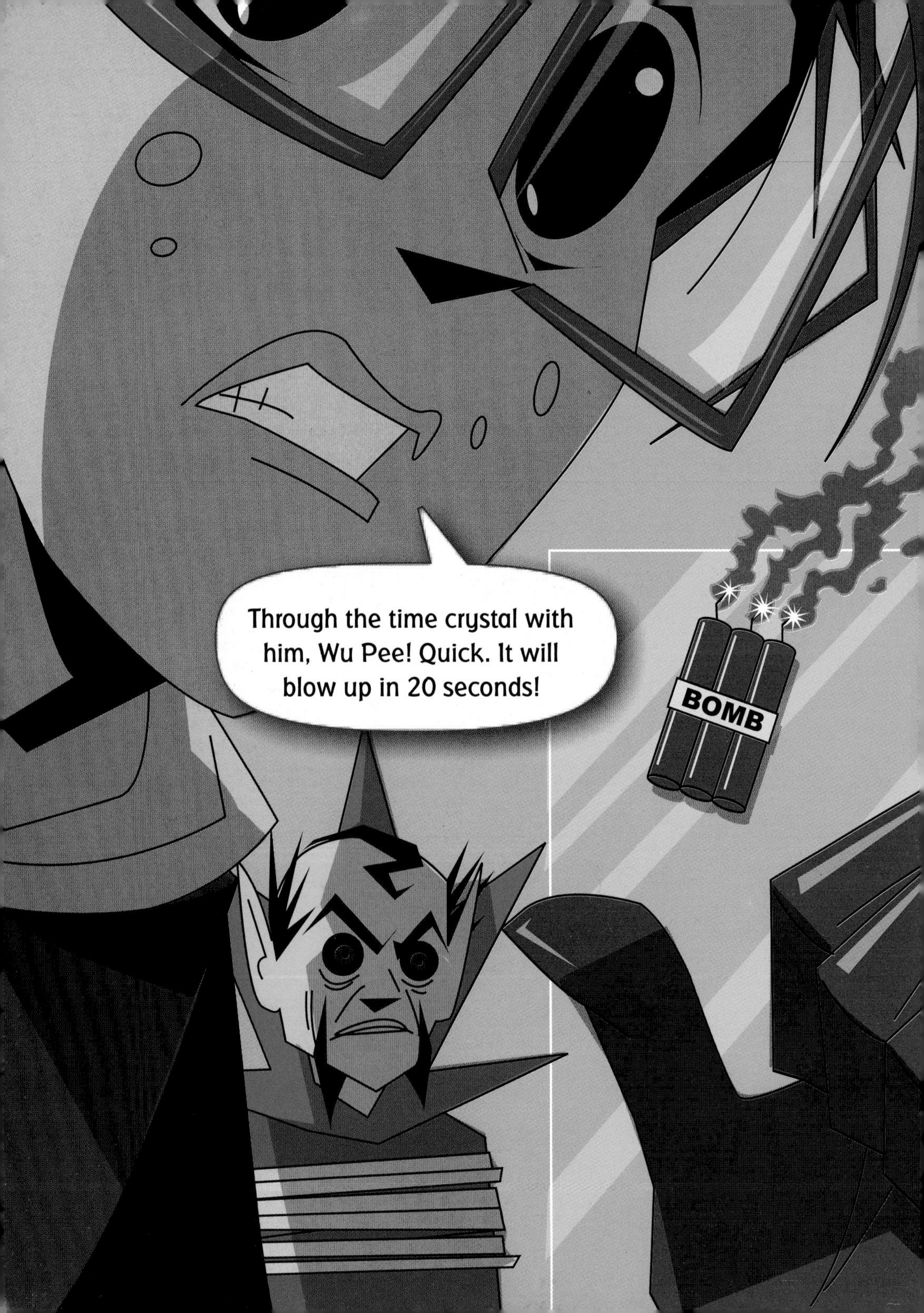
Through the time crystal with him, Wu Pee! Quick. It will blow up in 20 seconds!
BOMB

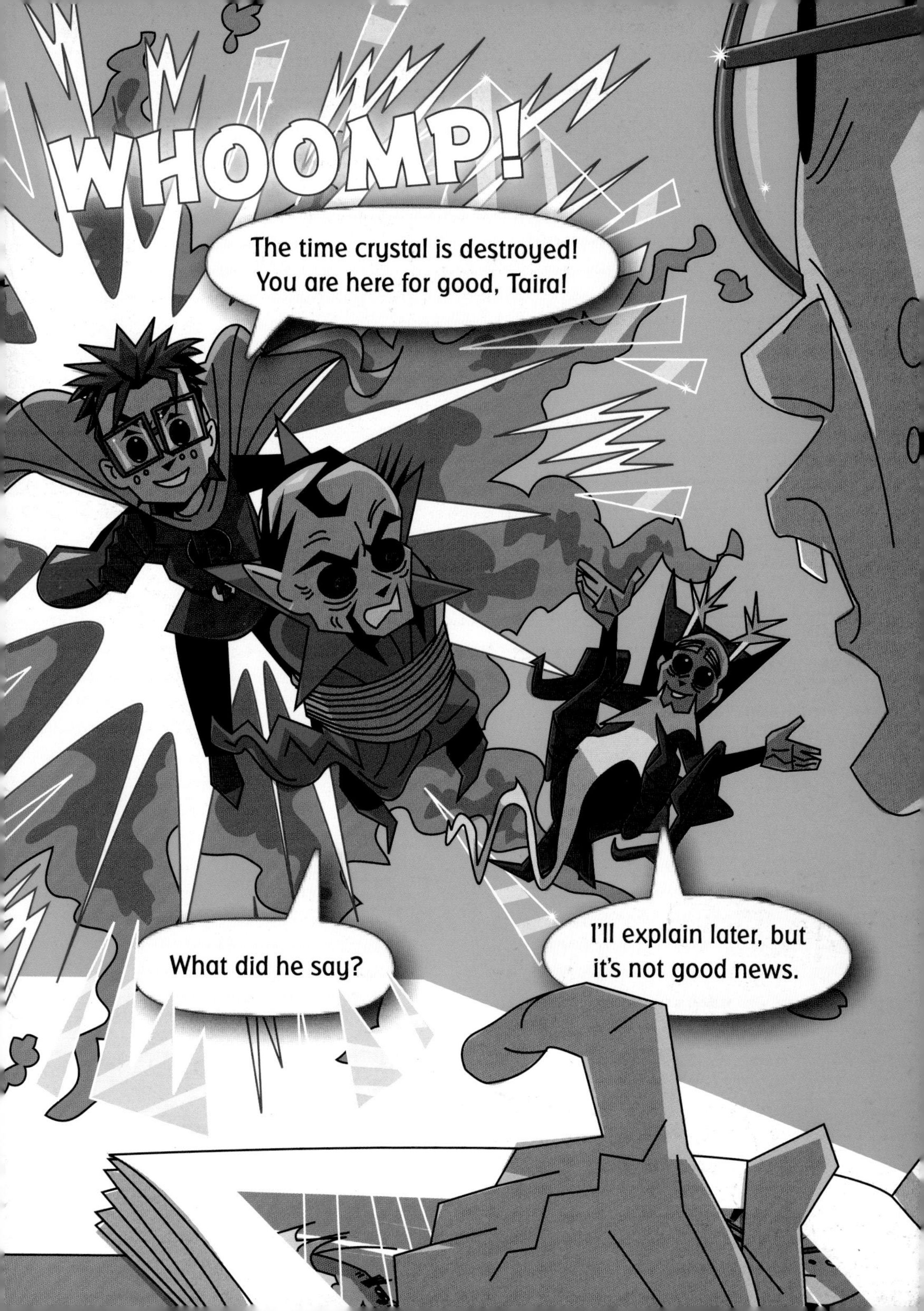
WHOOMP!
The time crystal is destroyed! You are here for good, Taira!
What did he say?
I'll explain later, but it's not good news.

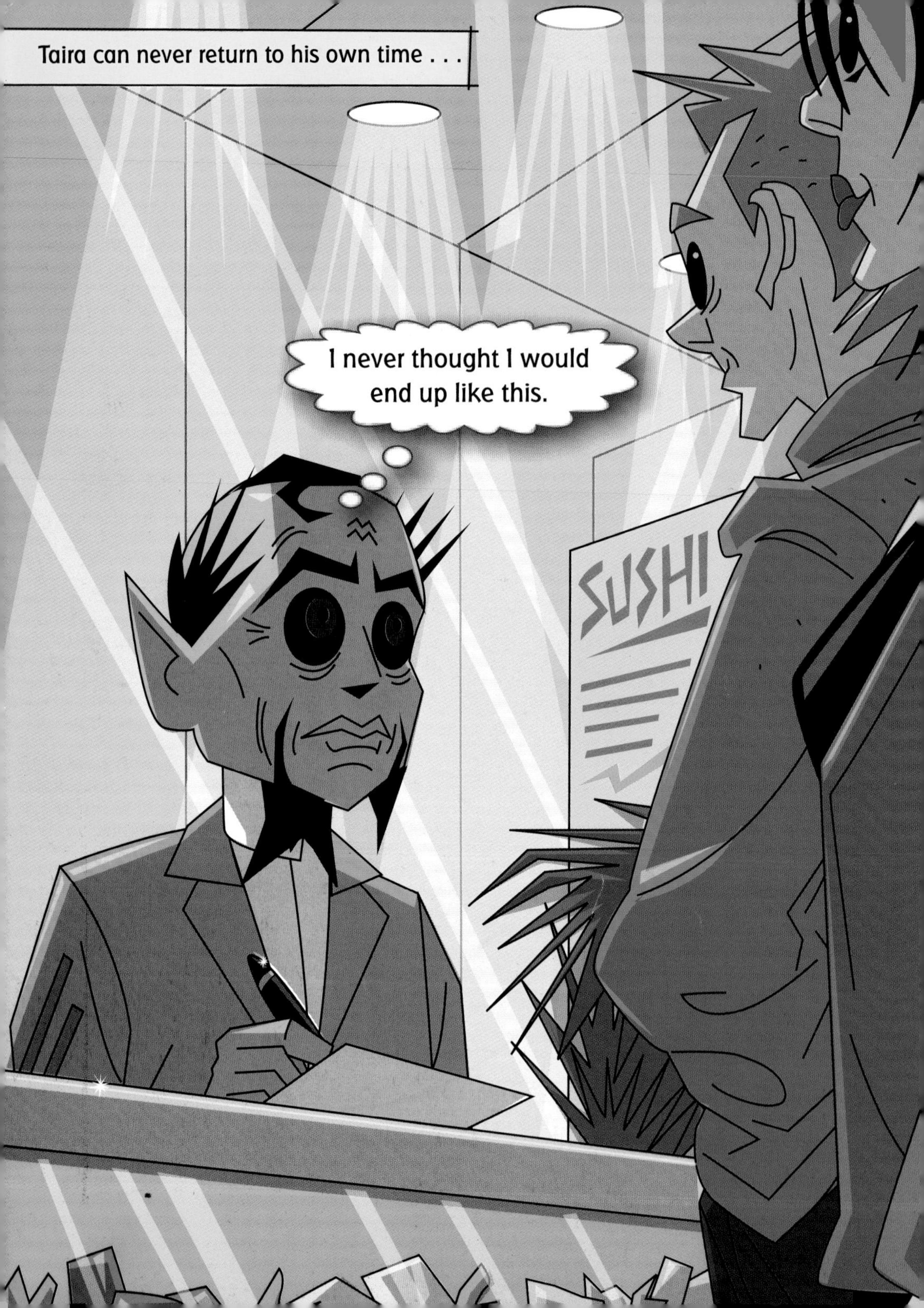
Taira can never return to his own time . . .
I never thought I would end up like this.
SUSHI

ABOUT THE AUTHOR

David Orme has written over 200 books
including poetry collections, fiction and
non-fiction, and school text books. When he
is not writing books he travels around the UK,
giving performances, running writing workshops
and courses.

Find out more at:
www.magic-nation.com.